ABOUT
AVERAGE

Also by Andrew Clements

A Million Dots

Benjamin Pratt & the Keepers of the School
We the Children
Fear Itself
Whites of Their Eyes
In Harm's Way
We Hold These Truths

Big Al
Big Al and Shrimpy
Dogku
Extra Credit
Frindle
The Handiest Things in the World
Jake Drake, Bully Buster
Jake Drake, Class Clown
Jake Drake, Know-It-All
Jake Drake, Teacher's Pet
The Jacket
The Janitor's Boy
The Landry News
The Last Holiday Concert
Lost and Found
Lunch Money
No Talking
The Report Card
Room One
The School Story
Troublemaker
A Week in the Woods

ABOUT AVERAGE

Andrew Clements
Illustrations by Mark Elliott

Atheneum Books for Young Readers
New York · London · Toronto · Sydney · New Delhi

atheneum

ATHENEUM BOOKS FOR YOUNG READERS

An imprint of Simon & Schuster Children's Publishing Division

1230 Avenue of the Americas, New York, New York 10020

This book is a work of fiction. Any references to historical events, real people, or real places are used fictitiously. Other names, characters, places, and incidents are products of the author's imagination, and any resemblance to actual events or places or persons, living or dead, is entirely coincidental.

Text copyright © 2012 by Andrew Clements

Illustrations copyright © 2012 by Mark Elliott

All rights reserved, including the right of reproduction in whole or in part in any form.

ATHENEUM BOOKS FOR YOUNG READERS is a registered trademark of Simon & Schuster, Inc.

Atheneum logo is a trademark of Simon & Schuster, Inc.

For information about special discounts for bulk purchases, please contact Simon & Schuster Special Sales at 1-866-506-1949 or business@simonandschuster.com.

The Simon & Schuster Speakers Bureau can bring authors to your live event. For more information or to book an event, contact the Simon & Schuster Speakers Bureau at 1-866-248-3049 or visit our website at www.simonspeakers.com.

Also available in an Atheneum Books for Young Readers hardcover edition

Interior design by Mike Rosamilia, jacket design by Russell Gordon

The text for this book is set in Bembo.

The illustrations for this book are rendered in pencil.

Manufactured in the United States of America

0314 OFF

First Atheneum Books for Young Readers paperback edition April 2014

10 9 8 7 6 5 4 3 2 1

The Library of Congress has cataloged the hardcover edition as follows:

Clements, Andrew, 1949–

About average / Andrew Clements ; illustrated by Mark Elliott. — 1st ed.

p. cm.

Summary: As the end of sixth grade nears, Jordan Johnston, unhappy that she is only average in appearance, intelligence, and athletic ability, reveals her special skills when disaster strikes her central Illinois elementary school.

ISBN 978-1-4169-9724-5 (hc)

ISBN 978-1-4169-9725-2 (pbk)

ISBN 978-1-4169-9726-9 (eBook)

[1. Ability—Fiction. 2. Schools—Fiction. 3. Individuality—Fiction. 4. Heroes—Fiction. 5. Tornadoes—Fiction.] I. Elliott, Mark, 1967- ill. II. Title.

PZ7.C59118Abo 2012

[Fic]—dc23   2012015106

For Tara Howard
—A. C.

CHAPTER ONE

CERTAINTY

It was a sunny spring morning, but there was murder in the air. Jordan Johnston was killing *Pomp and Circumstance*. Actually, the whole elementary school orchestra was involved. It was a musical massacre.

But Jordan's violin was especially deadly. It screeched like a frightened owl. Mr. Graisha glared at her, snapping his baton up and down, side to side, fighting to keep all twenty-three students playing in unison. It was a losing battle. He glanced up at the clock and then waved both arms as if he needed to stop a freight train.

"All right, all right, stop playing—everyone, stop. *Stop!*" He mopped his forehead with a handkerchief and smiled as best he could. "I think that's enough for this morning. Don't forget that this is Thursday, and we have a special rehearsal right

1

here after school—*don't* be late. And if you have any free time at all during the day, please *practice*. We are *not* going to play well *together* if you can't play well *by yourself*, right? Practice!"

Jordan put away her violin carefully. She loved the instrument, and she was very good at putting it away. She was also good at polishing the rich brown wood and keeping the strings in tune, and keeping the bow in tip-top condition. It was playing the thing that gave her trouble.

But she was *not* going to give up on it.

She had given up on so many things during the past eight months. The violin was her last stand, her line in the sand. She was bound and determined to become a gifted violinist—instead of a scary one.

She was still a member of the sixth-grade chorus, but she didn't feel that was much of an accomplishment. Every other sixth grader was in it too.

Jordan wasn't shy about singing. She sang right out. She sang so loudly that Mr. Graisha had taken her aside one day. He was in charge of all things musical at Baird Elementary School—band, orchestra, chorus, everything.

"Jordan, you have great . . . enthusiasm. But it would be good if you didn't sing louder than all the other kids around you. The audience needs to hear them too, don't you think?"

Jordan got the message: *Your* voice isn't so good.

She almost always sang the correct notes, she was sure of that. She wasn't a terrible singer—just not good enough to be the loudest one. Her voice was about average.

Her friend Kylie had a gorgeous voice, high and sweet and clear—but she was so timid. Kylie barely made a squeak during chorus practice, and she hardly whispered at concerts. It drove Jordan crazy.

She wanted to grab her by the shoulders and shake her and shout, "Kylie, if *I* had a voice like yours, I would already live in Hollywood—no kidding, I would be a *star* by now! What is *wrong* with you?"

Jordan was a careful observer of all the talented kids at her school—the ones who got the trophies and awards, the ones who were written up in the local newspaper, the ones who were obviously going to go on and do amazing and wonderful things all the rest of their lives. *They* were the gifted ones, the talented ones, the special ones.

And she was not one of them.

After her violin was tucked safely into its bulletproof case, Jordan began putting away the music stands. She carried them one by one and stacked them over in the dark corner of the stage next to the heavy folds of the red velvet curtain. When all twenty-three stands were arranged neatly, she folded the metal chairs and then stacked each one onto a rolling cart. She also tipped Mr. Graisha's heavy podium up onto its rollers and wheeled it over to its place next to the grand piano.

It was already warm in the auditorium, and she leaned against the piano a moment. Moving that wooden podium always made her feel like a weight lifter, and she didn't want to start sweating so early in the day. It had been hotter than normal all week long.

Jordan had volunteered at the start of the school year to be the orchestra stage manager. She arrived early for each rehearsal and set up the chairs and the music stands. Then, after rehearsal, she stayed to put them all away again.

She didn't do this to get on Mr. Graisha's good side—the only sure way to do *that* was to be a super-talented musician. She just liked helping out. She also liked the stage to be orderly. She knew how to arrange the chairs and music stands correctly, and she understood how to put everything away again, just right.

Her best friend, Nikki Scanlon, had wanted to be the co-manager, but Jordan enjoyed doing the work herself. Also, by the time she finished putting things away three mornings a week, Jordan was sometimes by herself, alone on the big stage. She enjoyed that, too.

And today, like the other times she'd been alone in there, she went to the center of the stage and looked out over all the empty seats.

Baird Elementary School had once been the town's high school, and the auditorium was in a separate building off to one side. It was a large room. Row after row of theater seats sloped up to the back wall.

Jordan smiled modestly and walked to the front edge of the stage. Looking out over the crowd, she lowered her eyes then took a long, graceful bow.

The people were standing up now, whistling and hooting and clapping like crazy. She smiled and bowed again, then gave a special nod to her mom and dad, there in the front row. She even smiled sweetly at her big sister, Allie, and her little brother, Tim. Of course, Tim didn't notice. He

was only four, and he was staring at the blue-and-red stage lights with one finger stuck in his nose.

A young girl in a blue dress ran down the center aisle from the back of the hall, stretched up on tiptoes, and handed Jordan two dozen yellow roses—her favorite flower. With the bouquet cradled in one arm, Jordan took a final bow and backed away. The red velvet curtain parted for just a moment, and she slipped backstage.

There were people asking for autographs, plus some journalists with their cameras flashing, and a crush of happy friends, eager to congratulate her and wish her well. It was wonderful, and Jordan savored each second, as she had so many times before.

Brrnnnnng!

The first bell—six seconds of harsh, brain-rattling noise. It echoed in the empty auditorium. Outside behind the main building, kids whooped and yelled as they ran from the playground and lined up at the doors.

The intruding sounds did not touch Jordan's joy and certainty. She felt absolutely sure that one day her moment of triumph would be real, a part of her life.

But why would all those people be applauding *her*? She had no idea.

CHAPTER TWO

PRETTINESS

Jordan's memory was a powerful force. A moment from the past would sneak up and kidnap her and then force her to think about it until she discovered something she didn't know she knew.

On this particular June morning, a thought grabbed her as she pushed open the heavy stage door and began walking to the main school building. She remembered a book she had read near the end of fifth grade.

It was a famous one, *Sarah, Plain and Tall*, and for a couple of days there, Jordan had wished her mom was dead. Not really. But that's what had happened in that story, and it caught her imagination.

This dad lived with his daughter and son, and they all felt sad because the mom had died. But there was a woman, Sarah, coming to visit, and she *might* become the dad's new wife—a new mom.

It was deliciously sad. Jordan loved sad stories.

Jordan also loved this woman in the book right away, this Sarah. She was plain, and she knew it, and she didn't try to hide it from anybody. She even came right out and said it to the man who might become her husband: *I'm plain. And tall.*

Jordan was plain too. That's what this memory was forcing her to think about.

But it wasn't like being plain was some new discovery for Jordan. She had always known that. She was plain, but, unlike Sarah, she wasn't tall. She wasn't short, either.

She was Jordan, Plain and Average.

Being pretty and being tall were two of the ways Jordan did not feel special, and they both felt important. Especially prettiness.

Her face was her face, and there wasn't much she could do about it.

Of course, she had seen TV shows about how women could change their faces. And sometimes a woman looked better afterward . . . sort of. Except she never looked quite like *herself* anymore.

Jordan couldn't imagine ever doing that. She had a smaller version of her dad's nose, and she knew she'd miss that if it went away. Also her mom's eyebrows. Jordan knew she wasn't going to be famous for her beauty. And she was okay with that . . . until she started thinking about boys.

There was one particular boy, Jonathan Cardley. He played cello in the orchestra. As Jordan walked toward the main school building that morning, she spotted him with his friends over near the playground doors.

Jonathan had straight brown hair. Sometimes it hung down a little too far onto his forehead and covered his eyes, which she didn't like. They were nice eyes, a greenish-blue color. He was taller than most of the other sixth-grade boys, and Jordan thought he always looked good, no matter what he was wearing. He looked especially good when he wore jeans and a white collared shirt, like today.

Jonathan seemed to care a lot about prettiness. Most of the time he only talked to the nicest-looking girls—including Kylie, her friend with the gorgeous voice.

But at least Jonathan knew who Jordan was. He even talked to her now and then. He would say, "Hey, Jordan—have you seen Kylie?"

Kylie, Cute and Tall.

Jordan wished that all the really pretty girls

would disappear, one by one, until *she* was left as the cutest girl at school. Then Jonathan Cardley would be asking some other girl, "Hey, have you seen Jordan?"

A lot of girls would have to vanish.

Jordan pulled open the heavy door at the end of the walkway, took a left, and headed for the sixth-grade hall. It was a separate part of the school because all the sixth graders switched classes this year, just like they would next year at the junior high.

Jordan wasn't looking forward to homeroom today. She never looked forward to homeroom.

Kylie would be there, same as always, but she wasn't the problem. Ever since they'd become friends during fourth grade, Kylie had never said one mean word, never teased her about a single mess-up, never made her feel plain or untalented or awkward.

Kylie, Kind and Cool.

And Kylie had been nice to her when they'd been on the sixth-grade soccer team back in September and October, and then during basketball season, too. Of course, Kylie had been a star on both teams—Kylie, Strong and Skilled.

No, the problem with homeroom wasn't Kylie. The problem was . . . *someone else.*

Jordan did not want to even *think* the name.

Because this had been a good day so far. Yes, it was too warm, but it was bright and sunny, and it was one day closer to summer vacation. And the best part of the day so far? She had managed to avoid *that person* during orchestra practice. Now, if she could just make it through homeroom without any contact, then they'd be in different classes until gym.

As Jordan went toward the sixth-grade hall, she made herself walk more slowly. She also planned to stop into the girls' room. She wanted to arrive at homeroom just as the bell rang. She did not want to spend one extra second anywhere near *her*.

CHAPTER THREE

FURIOUS

It was hard to believe that one medium-size sixth-grade girl could express so much anger without saying a word. But it was happening. Jordan Johnston was radiating massive waves of negative energy, a huge force field of harsh, burning rage. And on this beautiful June morning, it took almost everyone in her homeroom completely by surprise, especially Mrs. Lermon.

Because normally, Jordan Johnston was a dear. She was also a sweetie, a love, a treasure, and a little darling. All her teachers said so, and they'd been saying so ever since first grade.

Jordan was a love because she never broke any rules. She was a treasure because she usually had a smile on her face. And she was a little darling because she always worked up to the very best of her abilities. Her grades were never great, but she earned those grades cheerfully, with good old-fashioned hard work.

That had always been part of Jordan's charm—nothing seemed to come easily for her, but she worked hard anyway. She kept focused on her own business, and she didn't demand a lot of attention.

Mrs. Lermon secretly wished she could clone Jordan, because if even *half* of the other children were even *half* as sweet, then the whole school year would be so much . . . nicer. Mild and pleasant, quiet and orderly, careful and attentive—*that* was the Jordan Johnston all her teachers knew.

Not today. The clouds of bitterness and anger on her face were startling, almost frightening—which Kent Donley learned the hard way. He needed to borrow a pencil, so he tapped her on the shoulder.

Jordan spun around, her eyes narrowed to slits.

"What?" she snapped.

"Uh . . . never mind," Kent whispered, backing away to a safe distance.

Imagine a sweet little goldfish that has always swum happily around and around in its bowl, and then one day a boy reaches down to drop it a pinch of breakfast, and the thing suddenly has razor-sharp teeth and leaps up and tries to bite off his arm.

That was how Kent felt. It was quite a shock, and Mrs. Lermon saw it all.

After the Pledge and the announcements and attendance, homeroom was quieter than usual. Jordan sat there in the third row, staring straight ahead, her lips pressed together into a tight line. She was like a steaming volcano, a cauldron of hot lava. Plenty of people were curious, but no one wanted to risk getting scorched, not even her teacher. They all left her alone.

If her friend Nikki had been around, she'd have pulled Jordan out of her foul mood. She was good at that. She never let Jordan take things too seriously. She'd have tickled her or made faces or stood on her head—anything to make her laugh a little. But Nikki was down the hall in Mr. Stratton's homeroom, so Jordan seethed and simmered for the whole sixteen minutes.

When the bell for first period rang, Jordan sat still while the room emptied around her. Then she stood up, jerked her book bag to her shoulder, and headed for the door.

Mrs. Lermon felt like she ought to say something helpful to the poor child.

"Jordan . . . ?" she began.

Jordan turned, and her fierce scowl stopped the teacher cold.

Mrs. Lermon gulped. "Um, have a nice day, okay?"

Jordan started to say something back, but she caught herself—which was probably a good thing. She clamped her jaw shut and stalked out.

CHAPTER FOUR

THREE MINUTES

I n the history of Jordan's day so far, only about three minutes have not yet been accounted for. Three minutes is not a long time, but sometimes it's long enough to change a goldfish into a barracuda.

Those three missing minutes were spent in the girls' room, the stop Jordan made just before homeroom. Marlea Harkins was in there. Lindley, Kathryn, and Ellie were there too, but they were not the problem. The problem was Marlea. She was that *someone else*, the person Jordan had been trying to avoid all morning.

And what did Marlea do when Jordan went into that bathroom? Well, first, there was something that had happened two days before.

On Tuesday morning Jordan had been cleaning out her notebook during homeroom, getting rid of some old papers. She had dumped a thick stack into the recycling bin.

Marlea had been watching, and she slid over to the bin and gathered up all that paper. She wanted to look through it to see if Jordan had thrown away anything that might be . . . interesting.

And she had found something.

What Marlea had found . . . well, there was something *else* that had happened two months earlier during a social studies class.

On that particular April afternoon, Mrs. Sharn had pushed the button on the DVD player. The screen had lit up, and sound filled the classroom—thundering hoofbeats, clanging swords, and the piercing call of a trumpet. A narrator began talking, and all the kids in the room started taking notes about the Peloponnesian War—everyone except Jordan Johnston.

Jordan was fighting a battle of her own that afternoon. She was working on a list—actually, three lists on one sheet of paper: Thing I'm Great At; Things I'm Okay At; Things I Stink At.

Her "Okay At" list was the longest: drawing, singing, running, swimming, telling jokes, dancing, soccer, basketball, lawn mowing, bubble gum bubbles, baking cookies, football, bicycling, spelling, making pizza, reading maps, knowing bird names, folding clothes—the list went on and on, naming more than thirty different activities.

Her "Stink At" list was also fairly long: math, playing violin, Frisbee, softball, ice skating, bowling, Ping Pong, memorizing, saving money, knitting, potholder weaving, sewing, chess, jigsaw puzzles, crossword puzzles, computer games, computers, science projects, tennis, piano, opening jars, washing dishes—and more.

But her "Things I'm Great At" list was the worst—only two things: babysitting and gardening.

Jordan frowned at herself that morning, thinking hard. There *had* to be other things she was really good at. . . .

At that moment Mrs. Sharn had stood up and walked to the rear of the room, glancing around to be sure everyone was taking notes. Jordan hid the paper under her notebook and lifted her eyes to the screen. She put an expression on her face that showed how much she loved studying the Peloponnesian War, then bent over and acted like she was writing.

When the teacher sat back down, Jordan quickly added an item to the "Great At" list: *pretending I like ancient history*. Then she made a face and added another thing: *making lists*. And then she added *actually learning history* to her "Stink" list.

Feeling guilty, she hid the paper again and gave the TV program her full attention. All around her, kids were scribbling away, writing down details that would probably be on tomorrow's quiz. After fifteen seconds Jordan began losing interest in the Greeks, and a minute later she was looking at her three lists again.

She sighed. Her "Great At" list was just terrible. . . .

Well, she thought, *but to have so many different things I'm okay at? That's pretty good. . . .*

She sighed again. She knew she was kidding herself.

The people who were okay at dancing? Those were the ones who got voted off the big TV show, the ones who never made it to Las Vegas, the ones who got sent back home . . . to Illinois.

And the "okay" singers? Same deal—no trip to Los Angeles, no million-dollar prize, no recording contract. Only a one-way ticket back home to Loserville. In Illinois.

Just being *okay* at things did not feel okay. Not at all.

And as Jordan sat there thinking how awful and

miserable her life was, Mrs. Sharn made it worse.

She paused the DVD. "We're going to have a quiz on the part of the program you just watched—you may use your notes."

Jordan quickly stuffed that paper with the lists on it into her notebook. She tried to recall some of the things the narrator of the program had been saying . . . but memorizing facts was on her "Stink" list.

The quiz was a disaster. There were ten questions, and she knew the correct answer to only one.

After that class Jordan hadn't really wanted to look at those lists anymore. In a week or so she'd moved on to other worries, and she didn't notice that single piece of paper among the old stuff she had dumped into recycling on Tuesday.

And all that led Jordan back to Thursday morning in the girls' bathroom just before homeroom. She stood in front of a sink, paralyzed with embarrassment, as all three of her private lists were read out loud, very dramatically.

The entire performance took Marlea Harkins less than three minutes.

CHAPTER FIVE

TWO GOOD THINGS

Jordan was still fuming when she sat down in her first-period class, but there were two good things about intermediate math. First of all, Marlea wasn't there; and second, Jonathan Cardley was.

But even seeing Jonathan sitting just one row over and one seat ahead didn't make her happy this morning.

Marlea Harkins.

Jordan clenched her jaw tighter. She tried to aim her thinking somewhere else, *anywhere* else, but she couldn't.

What she hated most? Feeling like she really *hated* someone. Jordan kept fighting that feeling— just as she had all year long. But Marlea didn't make it easy. The girl was just so *mean*.

"If you can't say something nice, don't say anything at all."

That was her mom's voice inside Jordan's head.

Her mom said that a lot, especially when Jordan and her sister started arguing.

Well . . . all through homeroom today, and really, all year long, she hadn't said a single "not nice" word to Marlea—at least, not out loud. . . .

"If you can't *think* something nice . . ."— Ha! Think something nice about that . . . that *creature*? No way!

And now that Marlea had those stupid lists? It was like an enemy general suddenly had a perfect map of all the weakest places along her borders, all the easiest spots to attack. And she would. She would come at her again and again—just as she had all year long.

But Marlea was careful. The anti-bullying program was a big deal in Salton, Illinois.

Even though Jordan was pretty sure she had enough evidence to file a complaint with the guidance counselor, what could Mr. Lifton do? Yes, he would call in Marlea and her parents, and he would call in Jordan and her parents, and then Jordan would have to try to prove how Marlea had been taunting and teasing, and how she made other kids laugh at her, and how Marlea went out of her way to bother her.

And if she did all that, what would it accomplish? Would Marlea be punished? Probably. Would Marlea become any nicer? Probably not—just sneakier and meaner. It would make Marlea hate her even more. Because it wasn't like Marlea was going to get sent away to some bully reform school or move out of town or something. She'd still be around.

And would that long anti-bullying process make *her* stop feeling like she hated Marlea, make all of her Not Nice thoughts stop? That was the question that bothered Jordan most.

Because this situation with Marlea? It wasn't like in fourth grade when those two guys kept punching her friend Henry on the bus. Henry turned them in, and the bullying stopped, and the whole anti-bullying process worked just like it was supposed to. This felt different. She didn't feel threatened or like she was in danger . . . mostly she felt stuck. And trapped. And puzzled.

Also, Jordan felt that if she turned Marlea in to the school authorities, that would make *her* feel even worse. It would be one more thing to add to her "Stink At" list—dealing with a mean kid.

No, somehow she had to get past it . . . or over it, around it, above it, through it, beyond it, between it . . . Jordan ran out of prepositions.

One thing was for sure. The first job she had to do today, right now, was *stop* feeling so angry. So just as the bell rang, Jordan made herself take a deep breath, and then another.

And as she pulled in that second deep breath, she was pretty sure she caught a whiff of the deodorant Jonathan Cardley was wearing. Or maybe it was cologne . . . or shampoo. Whatever it was, it smelled good, and Marlea Harkins vanished from her thoughts.

Jonathan Cardley was as average at math skills as Jordan was, so the two of them met up in room 117 every morning at 8:58. Jordan liked to think of it as sort of a first-period date—"Hey, I'll see you at Mr. Stratton's Intermediate Math Café!"

It was never much of a date. But Jordan always enjoyed herself anyway. Jonathan sat so close. And today as the class began checking the homework, Jordan sneaked about twenty looks at him.

He was chewing the end of his pencil, which he did a lot. He also had this special way of scrunching up his face whenever he worked on a word problem. And he liked to draw cars and trucks on the edges of his papers, and he bounced his right leg up and down a lot, and sometimes he chewed his

thumbnails. Jordan could have written a detailed article for a nature magazine: "The Habits, Plumage, and Migration Patterns of Jonathan Cardley."

As she glanced at him again, she thought, *Another good thing about intermediate math? Nikki's not here.*

Nikki was in the advanced math group, and she didn't like Jordan's fascination with Jonathan.

"I don't see why you think he's so wonderful."

That's what she always said. But Jordan knew it wasn't true—no sixth-grade girl could ignore Jonathan. Nikki just didn't want her to get her feelings hurt. She was just being a good friend.

Back in fourth grade, a couple kids in their classroom had teased Nikki about being adopted, and Jordan had helped put a stop to it. Jordan also invited her over for a sleepover—the first one Nikki had ever had. Ever since then Nikki had been her best friend, and also her self-appointed protector.

But math class was a Nikki-free zone, so she could enjoy the full Jonathan experience without getting teased about it later.

Sometimes she agreed with Nikki, though . . . because, really, what did she like most about Jonathan? She hated to admit it: his looks. She liked his *looks*. Which meant that *she* was just as impressed by prettiness as Jonathan seemed to be—maybe more. Handsome face, nice hair, beautiful eyes, great smile. He *wasn't* plain, and he *was* tall.

Jordan felt sure that Jonathan was also a good person, but truthfully? She probably would have still liked him even if she had proof that he enjoyed ripping the arms off of teddy bears.

Which she was sure he would *never* do.

That was more like something *she* might do.

That was something she actually *did* do, but she only did it once. And it was only because her big sister had pulled the head off her Barbie doll—after Jordan teased Allie about kissing Rob Velman on the front porch. On the lips.

Sitting there in math class, Jordan decided that all of her relationships were complicated.

But she hadn't meant to start thinking about herself. She wanted to keep thinking about her and Jonathan.

Except she knew there really was no "her and Jonathan." There was just her, wishing that there were.

CHAPTER SIX

HEAT AND NUMBERS

I am so hot!

Jordan fanned her face with one hand. She remembered hearing that in places like Texas and Florida and Southern California, all the schools had air conditioning. Not in Salton, Illinois. It was only a little after nine in the morning, and it was already more than eighty degrees in Mr. Stratton's classroom.

She didn't do so well when it got hot and humid. And today, the combination of actual heat, plus sitting near Jonathan, plus struggling with math problems, it all made her . . . well, there's no dainty way to say it. It made her sweat.

Her shirt was sticking to the back of her chair, her hair was sticking to the back of her neck, and her hand was sticking to the worksheet on her desk, wrinkling the cheap paper.

Sweatier and sweatier.

Then a memory swept into her mind—something that had happened right there in the same room, but after school. At chess club.

She'd been sitting over by the windows that day, and it was February, and Will Fennig faced her across the chessboard. After only three moves Jordan knew she was in trouble.

It had been cold that afternoon. A weather system had rushed down from Canada. It had licked across Lake Michigan, dropped a foot of snow on Chicago, and then kept charging south. By the time the air mass arrived in McLean County, it was nothing but pure, crackling cold.

The aluminum window frames inside the math room had been covered with frost, and Jordan hadn't worn a sweater. It was her move, and as she reached for her bishop, she shivered—and her hand knocked over Will's knight.

Quick as a weasel, Will jumped up out of his chair and shouted, "Hey! That's cheating!"

If Will had used his sharp analytical skills for half a second, he would have realized that Jordan certainly did not know enough about chess to cheat, even if she had wanted to—which she didn't.

Jordan had never cheated at anything. And if

she *had* ever wanted to, she sure wouldn't have wasted any criminal talent on something as pointless as winning a game of chess. She would have cheated for something real, like getting a free ticket to the Rotary Club's All-You-Can-Eat Spaghetti Supper.

She had joined the chess club to become a grand master. All the chess kids were super smart, and that's what she wanted to be. She desperately wanted to be respected for her brains—like the scarecrow in *The Wizard of Oz*.

After just two meetings of the chess club, Jordan felt certain that the game had been invented for the precise purpose of making her feel lost and stupid. It required a kind of thinking she just wasn't good at. She was able to see two or three moves ahead, but looking ahead seven or eight moves, like some of these kids could? Not her thing.

She wasn't sure if it was the cold, or how bad she felt about chess, or the squinty look on Will's face, or all three, but she completely lost it. She put both hands under the chessboard and flipped it upward so hard it that hit the light fixture. Plastic chessmen clattered to the floor as Jordan screamed, "You *win*! Happy?"

All eyes jumped to her, and she felt her face

glowing, first pink and then crimson. And the thought that came to her as she stomped out of that room?

At least I don't feel cold anymore!

The sweltering heat of that June morning pulled Jordan back to first-period math class. A bead of sweat ran down her forehead, along her nose, and dripped right onto her worksheet.

She quickly glanced over at Jonathan. He hadn't noticed, of course. Why would he?

She saw he was wearing his word-problem face. It occurred to her that with his average math-reasoning skills, he was probably as bad at chess as she was. And she had to admit, that thought made her very happy.

Then she also noticed how much Jonathan was sweating, and *that* made her even happier. They had so much in common—both of them were average at math, lousy at chess, and sweaty!

Maybe not the building blocks of a perfect relationship, but it was a start.

Sort of.

In her dreams.

Marlea Harkins . . . arrgh! That girl!

There she was, filling Jordan's mind again. She

could hear Marlea's voice, dripping with sarcasm, reading those lists out loud in the echoey girls' room.

Jordan had been tempted in there. She could have rushed over and tackled Marlea. She could have pushed her perfect little face down onto the grubby tile floor and grabbed that paper right out of her hand. That would have been *sweet*!

But she hadn't done it. Not because she didn't feel like it and not because she couldn't—she totally could have, she was sure about that. She probably outweighed Marlea by fifteen pounds.

Fifteen times two is thirty. Fifteen times three is forty-five. Fifteen times four is sixty. Sixty seconds in a minute. Sixty minutes in an hour.

Hours. Sometimes at night she lay awake for hours, a million thoughts running around in her head. And numbers rescued her. She would start counting backward, beginning at ninety-nine, thinking only about the numbers. And all the words and the thoughts were pushed out. . . .

Pushing Marlea to the floor? It just wasn't like her. She didn't do stuff like that. That was what a tough girl in some movie would do, or a kid on a TV show where something exciting has to happen before the next commercial or right at the end of the episode to make a bigger problem for next week's show. She had seen so many shows like that. She didn't want to be that way. It all seemed so fake, especially the mean stuff.

Because basically, I'm just a nice person . . . I am.

That thought almost embarrassed Jordan, but she knew it was true.

So . . . did that mean Marlea was basically a *nasty* person? Could that be true? It had certainly seemed that way this morning. . . .

Now, if Nikki had been there in the washroom? Things might have gotten rough. Nikki wasn't much of a forgiver-and-forgetter. She was more of a get-evener—fiercely loyal and deadly funny. She had the gift of sarcasm—or was it a curse? Jordan couldn't decide. Because Nikki could almost draw blood with her words. Even Marlea and her pals were a little scared of her—Nikki called them the Cuteness Club.

It was just as well Nikki hadn't been there. Jordan knew that this was *her* battle.

Deep down, some part of her also understood that *not* lashing out was her biggest protection—especially if she ever decided she needed to talk to Mr. Lifton. Because if she hauled off and whacked Marlea only *once*, or even just shoved her, that would ruin any possible anti-bullying case. Then *she* would look like the attacker—even if it was truly self-defense.

But more important than how it would *look*, there was her—just her. She wanted to stay who she was and not let Marlea or anybody else make her do or say anything outside that. She needed to keep herself herself.

Too many thoughts . . . a *fight*? She hadn't had a fight with anybody since kindergarten, and she certainly hoped she had gotten a little smarter since she was six!

Six times six is thirty-six, six times seven is forty-two, six times eight is forty-eight, six times nine is fifty-four . . .

Math was good sometimes—difficult, but good. Numbers were so clean and simple. No words, no feelings, no mind tricks. Numbers were like a hiding place, a quiet corner out of the wind.

Jordan was still hot, but only on the outside now. Today, math was the perfect thing.

And Jonathan? She sort of hated to admit it, but he was perfect too.

CHAPTER SEVEN

THE WEATHER BUSINESS

About fifteen miles away from where Jordan sat sweating in her math class, Joe Streeter was sitting in a cool, soundproof studio, talking into a microphone.

"Hey there, this is Joe the Weather Guy here at WCZF Radio 870—and I've got some good news, and I've got some bad news."

Joe said that same phrase every time he went on the air. It was always true, because if the weather was awful, it wouldn't last forever. And if it was a beautiful day, a worse one would be along soon. Good news, bad news.

Weather in central Illinois was serious business. Would the corn and soybeans take root, or would heavy spring rains rot the seed? Would the crop survive the summer, or would it get scorched or crushed by hail? When could the harvest begin?

Would the family still have a roof over its head next year?

The farmers in the area listened to Joe. Of course, anyone could get loads of weather information from TV, from the Internet, even from the phones in their pockets. But Joe was a homegrown weather guy. He grew up driving a tractor on his dad's land down near Heyworth, and he knew about McLean County farming from the ground up.

When he pushed that red ON AIR button, Joe always sounded bright and cheerful, but behind the jokey voice there was a weather scientist a person who studied his computer models, as if they held the secrets of life and death. Because once in a while, they did.

Earlier in the morning, Joe had been arguing with Warren Shane. Warren was the chief meteorologist at the National Weather Service office in Lincoln, Illinois, about fifty miles west and south of him.

"I grew up around here, Warren, and all I'm saying is it's just too darned hot and humid today, plus there's all that new-plowed land soaking up the sunlight. The numbers look wrong to me—I think we could have some trouble."

Warren was calm and patient. "I understand your concern, but the radar is fully deployed, Uncle Sam has the best supercomputers money can buy, and we're chewing on the data six ways from Sunday. Really, things look fine—and even if there was a problem, we'd have loads of time to snap out a warning. So relax. Have another cup of coffee, look out the window, crank up the air-conditioner, and tell the farmers over there it's going to be another great day to grow some corn. Okay?"

"Okay," Joe said, "you're the boss," which made them both chuckle as they hung up. Because Joe was making a joke. In the weather business, the only boss was Mother Nature, and she never let you forget it.

CHAPTER EIGHT

LATE BLOOMER

Jordan liked her reading class more than recess, even more than lunch. Reading was her best subject—the only one where she was in one of the top groups. And Mr. Sanderling was her favorite teacher because at least once a week he made everyone read silently for the whole period. Today was one of those days.

Hey—I should have put reading on my Things I'm Great At list!

But that idea made her think of Marlea, which she did *not* want to do. All she wanted to do now was read.

Jordan had been hooked on animal stories for a month or so. Mr. S. had some great ones in his classroom library, and not just newer books. He had a lot of his own books there on the shelves, the ones he had grown up with.

She'd found two inscriptions on the inside of an old hardcover copy of *The Black Stallion*: "For Jimmy, with love from Mother and Dad, Christmas 1953." And below that, another one: "For Tommy, with love from Dad and Mom, Christmas 1987."

She knew that Tom was Mr. Sanderling's first name, so her guess was that the book had probably first been a gift to *his* dad back in 1953.

Jordan imagined Mr. S. as a kid, finding a quiet place to curl up and start reading his new-old book on Christmas afternoon. The picture made her smile.

Books kidnapped Jordan the same way her memories did. Starting a new book was like jumping into a rushing stream—something she wished she could do right about then. She was still sweating.

But at least on hot days Mr. S. kept a fan running, a big old thing with black metal blades. It sat on a wooden stool at the front of the room, and each time it swung one way and started back the other, there was a soft *click*. It didn't make much of a breeze, but it was tons better than sticky stillness. And when she had to come back to Mr. Sanderling's room in the afternoon for seventh-period language arts? *Any* moving air was going to feel wonderful by then.

The whirring fan also blocked out most of the other sounds in the room. However, it did *not* block out the memory of Marlea's voice echoing around the girls' room. The sheer meanness of what that girl had done had burned itself into her mind. Not good.

But Jordan pushed back. She wasn't going to let a crowd of Not Nice thoughts about Marlea ruin her reading time. She'd just begun a new book about a girl who was a spy during the Civil War—and from the cover she could tell that the girl's horse was also an important part of the story.

Her dad loved reading too. He'd read to her almost every night when she was little, and later, when she wasn't so little, he kept it up. They had graduated to mysteries, biographies, adventure stories, spy novels—so many great books.

Spy novels . . .

A memory, something from back in the middle of December.

Jordan had heard her mom and dad talking softly in the family room, and then she'd heard her own name, so she'd thought they might be whispering about her Christmas presents.

She tiptoed closer for a little spying.

But they were talking about school. Jordan had just brought home her second report card—all Cs

and C minuses, with just one B. In reading.

"I'm worried, Jay." That's what her mom called her dad—his name was James. "Jordan's just not doing very well."

"Compared to what?" her dad said.

"Compared to all the other kids, of course."

"Her grades are average," he said. "Some kids do better than she does, some do worse. Nothing wrong with that."

"I just want her to do . . . better. That's all."

Jordan heard the worry in her mom's voice.

"She'll be fine," her dad said. "She's happy, she loves people, and her grades? They'll come along. She's just a late bloomer."

"But if she doesn't start getting better grades . . ."

"She's going to do just fine, sweetheart. We know she's a hard worker. That's ninety-five percent of success, right there. And life involves a lot more than getting good grades. So relax, okay? She's a good kid. We have to let her be herself."

Her mom sighed. "I'm just a big worrywart. You're right. I know you're right."

Jordan had backed away silently, feeling awful.

She'd gone to her room and flopped onto her bed. She lay there staring up at nothing. And a picture came to her thoughts—the vine that grew beside the arched gate into the backyard garden.

In March the vine was a few puny sticks in the ground next to the fence. By June it morphed into a leafy green canopy growing up over the arch, and by the end of August, it looked like a scene from a jungle movie—her dad actually used a machete sometimes to tame the dense foliage.

Then, near the end of September, only a few weeks before the first frost, there was a sudden explosion of tiny white flowers, hundreds of them covering the archway, and on still evenings a sweet perfume flooded the yard.

A late bloomer.

Her dad thought she was at the sticks-in-the-ground stage—not so great now, but good things would come. And her mom had sort of agreed.

So, do they talk and worry and argue about me all the time?

That was kind of a scary thought.

Still, she'd been glad to hear them say that stuff, to hear some unfiltered thinking on the subject of Jordan, Plain and Average.

They were always saying encouraging stuff to her one-on-one. But whenever her mom or dad talked to her directly, it felt sort of like a coach giving a pep talk. To a losing team.

The place her parents' conversation had ended up wasn't so bad. They didn't think she was a total loser. It was good to know they believed she was going to turn out okay . . . eventually.

Because most of the time, Jordan felt that way too.

She shook off the memory, opened her new novel to chapter three, and jumped right into the flow of the story.

But a part of her mind looked at what she was doing—reading this great book—and she compared *that* with what she'd been doing a minute earlier: worrying about her life.

The wonderful thing about reading this book? It had a sudden beginning and a burst of connecting episodes, and then it came to the end—and the ending was all worked out. Everything was so tidy, so nice and neat, packed between two covers. Read the words, turn the pages, and the ending was already figured out, just waiting for you to get there.

Reading this book was so *un*like living her life . . . but wasn't reading books actually a part of her living her life? And sometimes a *big* part of living it? Because she really did love to read. . . .

Too complicated.

Jordan shook her head free and switched off all the words in her mind—all except the new ones she was reading.

In less than ten seconds she even stopped noticing how warm it was.

CHAPTER NINE

SLIGHTLY WICKED

Reading ended, and Jordan did not want to go to PE. This was definitely going to be the hottest and sweatiest gym class since last September.

And of course, Marlea would be there.

But Kylie would too, so that was good. When Kylie was around, Marlea stayed on her best behavior, which was still pretty awful.

Best of all, Nikki would be there.

Jonathan would also be there, over on the boys' side of the gym—hidden, but still there.

Nikki was right. She really *was* thinking about him too much. . . .

And Mrs. Nevins would be there too, running the gym class. But not quite *really* running the class.

Mrs. Nevins. Another complicated relationship.

Jordan took a left at the drinking fountain and headed down the long hallway toward the gym. She'd been taking this walk every school day for years and years, but there had been a big change this last September. As she had started sixth grade, Mrs. Nevins had begun as the new girls' PE teacher at Baird Elementary. That was because over the summer, Mrs. Bellington had finally retired.

Mrs. Bellington had always made PE one of Jordan's best classes. The thing she liked most about Mrs. B.? She never criticized anyone for not being able to do something. Unlike Mrs. Nevins.

Jordan knew that she wasn't the most coordinated kid, and she knew she tended to get flustered in a team situation, when there was pressure to do something exactly right—like pass a ball so someone could score a goal. She also knew she didn't have the speed or endurance that some other kids did. But she had figured these things out on her own.

Mrs. Bellington had always told Jordan she was doing fine, that she was a good sport and a good team player, and that she was making progress. She never made her feel like there was something wrong with being an average athlete. Unlike Mrs. Nevins.

The first ten days of gym class under new

management hadn't been so great. Mrs. Nevins didn't give clear explanations about what she expected the kids to do, and then she was demanding and critical after they didn't do what she hadn't explained.

But when soccer season began, Jordan and Mrs. Nevins had gotten to know each other better. As Jordan turned the corner and went into the gym, she smiled, remembering how the soccer season had ended. She shook her book bag and listened for a soft metallic rattle, like a tiny jingle bell. . . .

Yup, it's still there.

The class hadn't begun yet, and she saw Kylie over by the bleachers hanging out with Lindley and Kathryn. And Marlea.

Oh, look . . . it's a meeting of the Cuteness Club! But Jordan bumped that little comment out of her head. That was definitely a Not Nice thought.

Kylie noticed her and smiled, then waved for her to come over.

The other girls didn't smile. Or wave. Or acknowledge she existed.

Jordan knew they didn't want her around, but she smiled and waved back at Kylie and walked over anyway. Which was sort of a Not Nice thing to do—but it was a free country, right?

As she joined the group, Marlea immediately turned her back. Jordan ignored the silent insult and said hi to the other three girls. Then she acted like she was paying attention to their chitchat.

But she wasn't listening. Her mind was months away—that ringy little rattle she'd heard from inside her book bag had sparked a memory.

Mrs. Nevins was also the girls' soccer coach. Back in November, when their amazing unde-feated season ended, all the other girls on the team had been awarded big gold trophies. Jordan had been given something else: an Acme Thunderer, a little silver whistle on a red ribbon.

Because the truth was, Jordan hadn't been on the team, not really.

She was *technically* on it at the very start, because anyone who tried out made the team automati-cally. Her soccer skills were okay, but she saw right away she wasn't going to be playing during any of the actual games. About fifteen girls were really good, and, of course, Kylie was one of the best. So was Marlea. And Nikki too.

Jordan didn't want to just sit on the bench and swat mosquitoes, so at the end of the second prac-tice, she had asked Mrs. Nevins if she could be her assistant. At first Mrs. Nevins thought that was sort of funny, but then she saw Jordan wasn't kidding.

She raised an eyebrow and gave Jordan a half frown, and then said, "All right—but only if you can explain what 'offsides' means."

So Jordan laid it all out perfectly, the complete offsides rule, which convinced Mrs. Nevins that she truly knew something about soccer. Because she did—just like she knew how to take care of her violin.

But Jordan knowing the rules of the game? That wasn't the kind of help Mrs. Nevins needed. Jordan could see that the woman was nine tenths of a mess, and she ran the soccer practices even worse than she ran her gym classes. She didn't seem to have an organized bone in her body. She brought her official clipboard and a pencil every day, but Jordan never saw her making notes or keeping track of anything.

The girls would show up and Mrs. Nevins would yell a few orders. Then after a little warm up, everyone just ran around, randomly kicking soccer balls all over the field. After about ten minutes of complete chaos, Mrs. Nevins would shout, "Okay, everybody! Choose up red and yellow vests—let's get a game going!" And that was soccer practice.

It was pathetic. The team needed structure. The team needed conditioning and basic drills. The team needed a plan. But there was no way Jordan could just start giving orders.

She began with little suggestions. She'd say, "Hey, Mrs. Nevins, should we maybe take ten minutes and use the cones to do some dribbling exercises before the scrimmage?"

And the coach would say, "Sounds good to me," and then yell out the order.

Or Jordan would say, "How about everybody does some wind sprints after the warm ups?"

And Mrs. Nevins would shrug and say, "Sounds good to me."

Jordan learned quickly that Mrs. Nevins didn't much care what the team did, as long as nobody got hurt and everyone stayed on the field until the late bus showed up at 4:05.

Jordan became Mrs. Nevins's planner, and in less than two weeks she was basically running the team. The coach still had the clipboard and the pencil, and she still yelled the orders, but nearly all the activities came from the worksheets Jordan printed up.

Practice began with stretching and exercises, followed by jogging and wind sprints. Then came drills—dribbling, tackling the ball, passing, inbounding, shots on goal, and corner kicks. Jordan made sure the two goalkeepers spent time defending the net. Each practice still ended with a game, but it was only about twenty minutes long.

When the Jefferson Jets showed up for the first match, the Baird Bumblebees crushed them, five goals to none. And the team just kept winning.

Kylie figured out Jordan had become the remote-control coach after about four days, and she thought it was great. Marlea figured it out after Kylie told her, and she did *not* think it was great.

And what did Jordan figure out during the soccer season? Whenever Kylie was the least bit nice to Jordan, it seemed to make Marlea crazy. Marlea needed to feel like she was Kylie's *only* friend. Marlea was jealous!

Which made no sense.

Because Marlea was pretty, she was a great student, a talented athlete, and she played cello nearly as well as Jonathan Cardley. So how in the world could a girl like *that* feel jealous of *her*—Jordan, Plain and Average? It was a mystery, and very annoying, especially during all those soccer practices.

So one October day after Jordan had put up with dozens of Marlea's snippy comments and hundreds of sideways looks and a million little frowny sneers, Jordan ducked around the corner of the field house out beyond the running track. She found those two concrete blocks that she had left loose and pushed them aside. She reached into the opening—yes, it was still there! She pulled out a slim aluminum case. She flipped the latch, opened the lid, and took out her nutrino-crux vaporizer. Jordan slid the nozzle around the corner, focused the viewer, took careful aim, and . . . *ffzzzt!* Marlea Harkins vanished above the soccer field in a pale-pink puff of perfumed smoke!

That wasn't Jordan's actual memory. It was wishful thinking—a Not Nice thought.

And slightly wicked.

Standing there now in the steamy gymnasium just before the bell rang that Thursday morning, she took a long hard look at Marlea, but not at her face—the girl still had her back turned to Jordan, trying to ignore her, trying to make her *feel* just how much she was hated.

And as Jordan kept on looking, it suddenly struck her that she was barely even seeing a *person* standing there. Because to her, Marlea had become less and less like a person and more and

more like one huge, ugly blob of bad memories. And who kept going back over and over all those bad memories and hurt feelings?

Me, myself, and I.

At that moment, Jordan saw how Marlea was actually doing something pretty useful for her. Yes, doing it in a mean and nasty way, but it was still useful. Because Marlea was forcing her to face up to that impatient, mean, and nasty part of *herself*—the part that wanted to whip out a vaporizer and start blasting.

Being nice to people would be so easy if the world were filled with Kylies. Being nice to someone like Marlea was a whole other thing.

Being nice to Marlea? Was that even possible?

The question hit Jordan like an electric current. Her heart actually began to pound.

And the next thought lit her up even brighter: *I should do that!*

Figuring out how to be genuinely *nice* to *that* girl? Even if she got meaner and meaner and meaner? *That* would be pretty amazing!

At the very least, it would mean taking niceness to some new level. It would require something way beyond your average, everyday niceness.

Because managing *not* to slug Marlea, or *not* to

rip out her hair, or *not* to turn her in to the guidance office for bullying—that wasn't really being nice. That was just *not* doing things she still *wished* she could . . . most of the time.

No, this new niceness was going to have to be made of steel—industrial-strength niceness. Awesome niceness. Award-winning niceness.

But . . . wouldn't this mean she'd have to forget about all those horrible things Marlea had been saying and doing all year long—truly *forgive* her?

That thought dumped a bucket of ice water on everything.

Jordan suddenly felt like the whole idea of being nice was dumb—like a crazy dream brought on by a fever. Maybe the only reason any of this had popped into her head was because it was so horribly hot today. . . .

But no matter how the idea had gotten into her mind, now it was definitely *there*. And all during the rest of gym class, she couldn't stop thinking about it.

CHAPTER TEN

NICED

Gym class turned out better than Jordan had thought it would. Mrs. Nevins didn't want anyone getting overheated or dehydrated, so she brought out equipment that she used with the really little kids—beanbag and ring-toss games, Hula-Hoops, and some foam Frisbees. She also wheeled out a cooler filled with little bottles of sports juice. There was no organized activity, so most of the kids just sat around on the mats and the bleachers, talking and sipping cold drinks.

Nikki had come rushing into the gym at the very last second—she was tardy a lot. She and Jordan ended up sitting in a corner near a big fan, tossing a beanbag back and forth.

Jordan thought about telling Nikki about her niceness idea. She tried to play it out in her head.

"So, I had this idea a few minutes ago."

"Yeah? What?"

"No matter what Marlea Harkins says or does, I'm going to be nice to her."

"Well, I think you should get the skinny little creep alone somewhere and tap her once, right on the nose—and I guarantee you, all these problems will stop. That's how I fixed a bully problem I was having in second grade out in California. Worked fast, worked perfectly."

Nikki had actually told Jordan about that—the way she'd dealt with a bully once. But she couldn't see herself punching Marlea. So they just tossed the beanbag and talked about plans for the summer vacation. But in the back of Jordan's mind, the new idea kept spinning.

By the time gym class was over, she'd decided that she'd creep up on this be-nice-to-Marlea thing—sort of phase it in over the next few days, maybe do a test or two to see if it had any chance of success—but only when contact with Marlea became unavoidable.

She still wanted to stay as far away from her as possible.

It turned out Jordan was not in charge of that. She and Nikki had stayed after class to help Mrs. Nevins put away equipment, so when they got to the cafeteria, they grabbed trays and went to the end of the lunch line.

Thursday was pizza day. The ovens had heated the cafeteria a good ten degrees hotter than the rest of the school, but the pizza was always good—completely worth some extra sweat. Jordan just hoped it wouldn't be all gone by the time she got to the serving counter. One thing she had learned about being late for lunch was that the milk down at the very bottom of the cooler was always the coldest, so that would be good.

As she slid her tray toward the food, a voice at her elbow whispered, "Hey, look! It's the *amazing* Jordan Johnston, that kid who's so *great* at *baby-sitting*!"

It was Marlea. She and Lindley were in line right behind her.

Marlea kept whispering. "Please—won't you tell me some of your fabulous *babysitting* tips? Because that's my dream—to get *great* at baby-sitting! Someday I want to be in the *babysitting* Olympics—because if you win a medal, you get a year's supply of free *diapers*. Please, please, please—won't you tell me the secret of all your thrilling *babysitting* success?"

The two of them were giggling and poking

each other now because of how hilarious they thought Marlea was.

Jordan wasn't usually good at put-downs, but a perfect reply flashed into her head: *A secret? Here's one: Never babysit for a completely stupid kid. Because once I had to deal with this really big baby named Marlea, and she got her huge head stuck inside the potty, and firemen had to come rescue her, and that sad little girl has not been able to say one nice word ever since—she turned into a real potty-mouth!*

Jordan didn't say that, but she knew if she wanted to test her niceness idea, she had to say something quick, before Nikki jumped into the mix.

Jordan turned to Marlea and smiled her warmest, sweetest smile. With her most sincere voice, she said, "You know, a lot of the things you say, they're like creative writing. You should work on the school newspaper at the junior high next year—really!"

And then she smiled again, turned back to her tray, and nudged Nikki to move ahead. Jordan took two quick steps and pulled a bowl of orange Jell-O off a glass shelf.

Marlea assumed Jordan was making fun of her. "Oh yeah?" she sneered, still whispering. "Well . . ."

But Lindley interrupted. "You should *totally* do that! Like, what if you made a gossip column for the paper—*oooh*, or maybe *fashion*!"

"Me?" Marlea said. "Don't be stupid!"

But Jordan could tell she felt flattered.

By then, she had the rest of her food. She paid and hurried away, leaving Marlea and Lindley arguing about which was better, juicy news or hot fashion.

Jordan followed Nikki to a table far away from where the Cuteness Club had settled, which was good. She didn't want Marlea to see her face. She knew she couldn't hide how surprised she felt.

Could something as simple as being *nice* actually work?

Too early to tell.

But still, hot pizza and cold milk had never tasted better.

CHAPTER ELEVEN

FORTS

W hat was all that noise about babysitting?" Nikki asked. She had finished eating. She always finished first.

So Jordan told her about the three lists and
how Marlea had gotten hold of them and what
had happened in the girls' room before homeroom.

"And babysitting was on my 'Things I'm Great
At' list."

"Hmm . . . ," said Nikki. "Along with what
else?"

Jordan wrinkled her nose. "Not much—actually,
only gardening."

"Well, that's dumb!" Nikki said. "You're great
at lots of stuff."

"Of course I am." Jordan smirked. "Like *what*?"

"Well . . . like being a friend. And always being

on time . . . and always doing all your homework, every single day. You're one of the only kids I know who always does every little bit of every single assignment."

"Except I get half of everything wrong," said Jordan.

"No, 'cause if you *really* got half of everything wrong, you'd be getting Fs, and you mostly get Cs. You're also great at taking care of animals. And horseback riding, too."

Jordan thought about that. Her dad wasn't a farmer, but they lived in an old house on about twelve acres of land a few miles outside of town. And they had a barn where they kept two ponies, Marge and Homer, and a quarter horse, a little mare named Cinders. They also had three sheep, four chickens, a rooster, and an old border collie named Shep. Most days, Jordan was the one who fed the animals, and she was the one who gathered up the fresh eggs almost every morning. She also groomed the horse and ponies, and she went out for a ride with Cinders at least once a week. She'd never taken riding lessons, but her mom had taught her to ride Western style starting when she was eight. And Nikki was right—she was really good at it now.

But there was something Jordan wouldn't say, not even to Nikki. She could barely think it to herself. None of the things she was great at *mattered*—at least not at school. The kinds of things she loved enough to be really good at? Those things didn't win awards or make her popular or make boys notice her. And now sixth grade was almost over—only a week left. Back in September, she'd made a big plan for this year, a plan that would send her off to junior high school in a blaze of glory, a flash of triumph, a burst of superstardom. It was brutally clear now that nothing had worked. Her whole sixth-grade year was a total failure. It was all so . . . disappointing.

Jordan sighed, but not loud enough to have to explain anything to Nikki.

"Well, anyway," she said, "because of those lists, Marlea thinks she's got a whole bucket of mud to throw at me. But I'm not going to react. I'm going to be *nice*, no matter what."

Nikki made a face at that. She had three brothers, two older and one younger, plus, she had moved to new schools four times since kindergarten. She had strong opinions about how a kid had to stand up for herself.

"So *that's* what you were doing!" she said.

"'Cause I was ready to smash a piece of cake into Snarlea's face. And I'll be happy to bonk her right on the nose for you anytime."

"Yeah," Jordan said, "and then get suspended. No, I want to do this my way. Or at least try it out enough to see what'll happen."

Nikki shrugged. "Suit yourself. I still think one good thump would do the trick."

They dropped off their trays and went outside. It was eleven fifteen now, and the harsh sunlight made them blink. The classrooms had been hot, the cafeteria had been hotter, but the playground won the prize. A light breeze wafted across the blacktop, but it didn't cut the humidity.

Walking toward the trees along the fence, Nikki said, "So, could you have answered that question Marlea asked? About secret tips for being a good babysitter?"

Jordan wasn't sure if Nikki was joking or not. She thought a second before answering.

"I do have a secret weapon, especially when I'm sitting for a toddler: build forts."

Nikki looked at her sideways. "Forts? That's the big tip?"

Jordan nodded. "Kids love making forts. And then playing in them. A table and a blanket, a couple of big cardboard boxes, two chairs and a bedsheet—you can make one out of almost anything. This kid named Jason Shermer and I, we made this great hideout from a coffee table tipped on its side near the back of a sofa, with four raincoats spread out for the roof and walls. And at the Carvers' house? There's a tall post at the bottom of the front stairs, and it's a perfect center pole for a teepee. So that's my answer: forts."

They sat under a tree, and the shade made the heat a lot more bearable. The grass was deep and soft from the recent rains, and Jordan lay back and looked up into the leaves overhead. She was tired of hearing herself talk, and she was pretty sure Nikki had had enough too. Talking took energy.

But she could have said a lot more about babysitting.

I really am *good at it.*

And *that* was something to be proud of—she was certain it was.

Babysitting took creativity. And kindness. And patience . . . and sometimes there were emergencies, like that time Bonnie Pershing started choking on a chunk of crayon. It popped out after one good whack on the back, but her lips had already started to turn blue. You really had to stay on high alert.

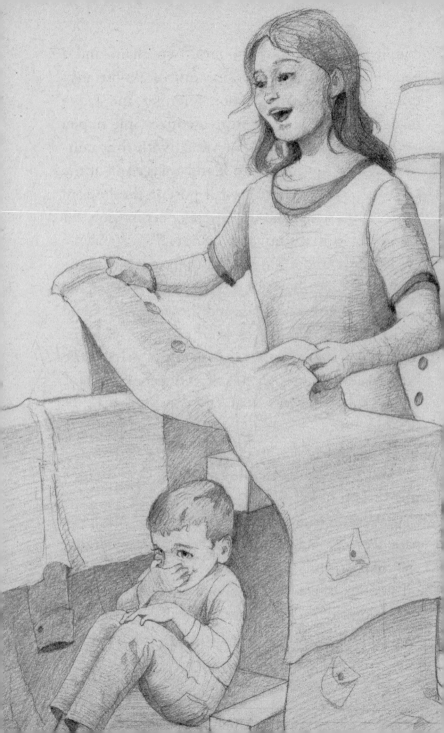

That night after the crayon incident she'd had trouble getting to sleep. Because what if Bonnie had kept on choking? And *died*?

No, babysitting wasn't a joke. But . . . that wisecrack Marlea had made about winning a medal and getting free diapers? That was actually pretty funny. . . .

Of course, diapers *were* part of the job. And cleaning up other messes too. Like when the Gottschalk twins dumped out five pounds of flour and then rolled around in it like it was snow.

But forts were good that way too, keeping kids busy.

And after building one, you could crawl in and play board games or draw pictures or read a story with a flashlight. And at nap time, toss in pillows, a stuffed toy, and a blanket, and the crankiest toddler in the world turned into a happy little camper.

Building forts—best babysitting tip ever. Definitely . . .

But thinking about that took her back to the cafeteria. That niceness thing back in the lunch line . . . Did that really work?

Or had it just *appeared* to work because it caught Marlea by surprise? It seemed kind of too good to be true.

One thing she knew from science was that it takes a *lot* of successful experiments to prove a theory is actually true, and she wasn't going to have much time for that. There was, after all, only one week left before vacation.

Still, there would also be all of next year to test the theory. Marlea wasn't going anywhere, and neither was she.

Looking up past the canopy of the tree, the sky was the most brilliant blue, with just a few handfuls of puffy clouds way up high, moving fast.

The days were moving even faster. It was hard to believe sixth grade would be over so soon. Then no more elementary school. *Ever.*

And in just a week, no more Marlea for the whole summer. The big niceness test would have to be put on hold for three months.

Of course, plenty could happen in a week. For that matter, a lot could happen in a single day—tons.

CHAPTER TWELVE

UPDRAFTS

Those same high, puffy clouds that Jordan saw above the school playground had gotten Joe Streeter's attention too. But he was looking at them in a different way. They made him worry.

Two things bothered him. First of all, any clouds at all could indicate a problem on a day like this. Clouds meant there might be updrafts—columns of hot, humid surface air being pulled straight upward.

The other thing he didn't like was how fast the clouds were moving. There were basic weather factors at work here. The jet stream was up there at twenty-five or thirty thousand feet, a giant river of air flowing from west to east, and moving fast—a hundred and fifty or even two hundred miles per hour. Which wasn't that unusual. But to have a polar jet stream dipping this far south right now? Not good. It caused instability in the upper atmosphere.

Plus, when you got up there four miles above the earth, the air temperature was about thirty degrees below zero. Cold air above, moving fast, and hot, humid air below—not really a problem, *unless* they started getting together.

Which led him back to those clouds. They might be evidence that columns of air had begun pulling heat and moisture aloft.

Joe had Warren's number on speed dial. He pushed the button and waited. It rang seven times, then went to voice mail: "You've reached Warren Shane, chief meteorologist at the NWS in Lincoln, Illinois. Leave a brief message, and I'll call as soon as I can."

Joe kept his voice calm and friendly, almost cheerful. "Hey, Warren, it's Joe again, over at WCZF radio. I wanted to get your take on those high cloud formations. The radar images aren't very clear at the moment, and I wondered if you had any other data. So give me a holler when you can. Thanks a lot."

Joe hung up and swiveled his chair back to the computer monitor, then clicked to refresh the radar image. During just the time he'd been on the phone, more clouds had bloomed.

No question about it. Conditions were changing.

CHAPTER THIRTEEN

GUTS

Art class ended before Jordan had finished the banner she was working on. She had sketched out all the letters, but only the C, the O, and the N were painted in. She was doing her very neatest work.

Miss Terkins had let everyone take it easy, and not just because it was so hot today. She had slacked off all week. They were too close to the end of the year to start any new projects, so they had begun making decorations for the sixth-grade graduation next Friday.

Sheesh—it's not like graduating is some huge deal!

Still, Jordan felt like everything was coming to an end.

That was what today's special after-school orchestra rehearsal was about too—getting ready for the graduation ceremony. The orchestra would play the march from Elgar's *Pomp and Circumstance*, and then the principal and the school superintendent would say a few words.

"This is not an ending; it's only the end of the beginning."

Jordan was sure stuff like that would be part of somebody's speech. She'd heard something similar at her sister Allie's sixth-grade graduation and then again at her eighth-grade graduation.

Kind of corny, but true.

And after the speeches, the principal would hand a certificate of completion to each of the sixth graders—that is, to everyone except Edison Raingle. Everyone knew that Eddie had to repeat sixth grade.

On days when she felt especially terrible about school, all Jordan had to do was remember how hard everything seemed for poor Eddie Raingle, and suddenly *her* life looked pretty good. The guy had so many problems.

It had made Jordan feel awful to think that way about him. And it had made her feel even worse one day when it had occurred to her that there were probably some parents who told their daughters, "Now, you'd better get to work, young lady, or soon you'll be worse off than that poor Jordan Johnston!"

So everyone except Eddie would be graduating.

And saying good-bye to all their teachers.

And leaving Baird Elementary.

Forever.

As Jordan washed out her brushes in the big sink, she realized that when she walked into the auditorium next Friday, she would look up and see CONGRATULATIONS! written in eighteen-inch-tall letters—letters that she had painted herself. It was sort of like baking the cake for your own birthday party.

When the bell rang for the next period, the sixth graders didn't burst out of their classrooms like they usually did. They oozed into the hallway and then trudged to their next classes, like weary prisoners moving from one cell to another. There wasn't much talking and almost no laughing.

Jordan looked at the thermometer on the wall outside Mrs. Lermon's science room: 86 degrees Fahrenheit, 30 degrees Celsius, 303.15 kelvin. And the relative humidity was 79 percent.

"Hey, watch it!"

"*You* watch it, idiot!"

Jordan turned around just in time to see Will Fennig slam Reed Addison against the lockers.

Mr. Sanderling rushed across the hall from his

doorway and stepped between them, both hands up like a traffic cop.

"Both of you, knock it off! Get to your classes, and not one more *word* to each other, or you'll both be in the principal's office, got it?"

Each boy nodded sullenly, and traffic in the hallway began moving again. Slowly.

Reed was at least a head taller than Will, and Jordan was surprised the smaller guy had been able to push the big one so forcefully, and that he had wanted to. They were practically best friends.

It had to be the heat.

It was business as usual in social studies. Three seconds after the bell rang, Mrs. Sharn said, "Take fifteen minutes and review pages 378 to 395 in your textbooks. Then we'll have a discussion about the main historical events during the reign of the Emperor Tiberius, beginning in AD 14. There will be a quiz on this material tomorrow or Monday. So take careful notes, particularly about the emperor's relationship with the Roman senate. Please open your books and begin. Now."

Jordan heaved a big sigh as she dug around for her book. Mrs. Sharn wasn't giving in. Not frazzled, frayed, distracted, or distressed—she didn't even look warm. She hadn't given up on her lesson plans, hadn't yielded an inch to either the heat or the end-of-the-year madness.

Well, I guess it's good that someone's trying to hold things together. . . .

But it did feel sort of pointless. Tiberius and the Roman senate in AD 14? How was knowing about *that* ever going to help her—unless she wanted to win at *Jeopardy!* on TV. Those people seemed to know everything. . . .

As she opened her book, a folded piece of paper sailed over her left shoulder and landed in her lap. It was a note.

She didn't react. Jordan didn't have to look to know who had tossed it. Social studies was a class that wasn't tracked—no high or low groups. And Marlea was back there, two seats behind on the left.

Once she felt certain Mrs. Sharn's attention was elsewhere, Jordan reached down and unfolded the paper, then smoothed it onto the right hand side of her book so she could read it.

I'm working on an article for the school newspaper next year: "What It's Like to Be a Total Loser." Can I set up a time to interview you?

Jordan felt the tips of her ears begin to glow.

No! She was *not* going to let herself feel insulted. Or angry. Or like she wanted to step back there, jam the paper into Marlea's mouth, and then make her chew it up and swallow it. No. *No.*

This was just another niceness test.

It was time to stay cool. Time to take a deep breath.

But what can I say or do that would seem nice?

If she replied with something like, "An interview? Sure, anytime," that might seem sarcastic—or stupid. Being nice didn't mean she had to pretend to be stupid.

Because I'm not. I'm not!

And in a flash, she had it. She knew what to write.

Jordan turned the note over.

Dear Marlea,
I'm sorry you think I'm a loser, because I know I'm not. But if you actually want to interview me, we could meet tomorrow after lunch. I'm sure it'd be interesting if we talked.
Sincerely,
Jordan

Quickly reading over her reply, Jordan almost tore it up. Who would believe someone who'd just been insulted could be that *nice*? It sounded fake.

She took a moment and read it again slowly, and this time she saw something different.

It was simple, really. Everything she'd written back to Marlea was true. She wasn't letting herself get mad or calling her an idiot, wasn't trying to win a point or get an advantage. She was just being honest and not letting hurt feelings get in the way. It was the kind of niceness that took some guts.

She refolded the note and tucked it into the palm of her left hand. She picked up her pencil, got up, and walked back to use the pencil sharpener near the door. When she was done, she retraced her steps and slipped the note onto the corner of Marlea's desk as she went past.

After that, Jordan put the whole thing out of her mind. She actually enjoyed reading about the conspiracies and power struggles in ancient Rome. It felt like a vacation.

CHAPTER FOURTEEN

WINNING

Jordan noticed that the fan in Mr. Sanderling's room was making that overheated-electric-motor smell. But the smoke alarm wasn't beeping, and the fan was still pushing the air around, still making its little click at the end of each turn.

Unlike Mrs. Sharn, Mr. Sanderling had pretty much given up on his lesson plans. Tests and quizzes and homework had been tossed out the window, and Jordan was happy about that. But the man was still keeping them busy. He'd served up a menu of little forty-three-minute projects all week. Today, his cheerful intensity was way too much.

"Okay, everyone, today we're going to write about something we all know very well, a common circumstance we each experience in our own unique way: this awful heat and humidity. Exciting, huh?"

The class answered with assorted groans and grumbles.

"And we are going to pour our thoughts on this topic into a very familiar, very compact little container: the haiku."

More groans.

"I know you all remember this small gem of poetic form: just three lines long, with five syllables in the first line, seven in the second, and five in the third. So simple, but so full of expressive possibilities. Any questions so far?"

Paul Ennis raised his hand, and Mr. S. nodded at him.

"Do we have to do this?"

"Yes, but I'm going to make it interesting."

More groans.

"This is a timed event—ten minutes. After ten minutes, anyone who wishes to compete for *a prize* may hand me one haiku. I will read each one aloud and assign it a number. After all entries have been read, I will read each one again, and each of you will vote for every poem, assigning a point value ranging from one to seventeen—one meaning not so great, and seventeen meaning terrific. Then we'll tally up the points, and the writers of the three top-scoring poems will win *the prize.*"

A chorus of voices: "What's the prize?" "What do we win?" "What do we get?"

Mr. Sanderling nodded wisely. "Here is a haiku answer:

> *"Excellent writers,*
> *cooler than autumn breezes,*
> *move to front of class."*

He pointed to his left.

"In plain English, the three top-point earners get to pull their desks up here and sit directly in front of the fan for the last fifteen minutes of the class. *Cool* prize, huh?"

More groans—a dumb pun.

Mr. Sanderling began passing out index cards. "Write your draft poems on your own paper, and when I call time, copy one fantastic haiku onto the card and put your initials at the bottom. And remember, you have to write about this weather."

Jordan's first thought was a lazy one.

So, really, I don't have *to do anything. . . .*

Which was true. Entering the competition was optional, and nothing was going to be graded. . . .

The room went silent. Some kids simply leaned forward and put their heads down on folded arms, and Jordan was tempted to take a little desk nap herself. She yawned, but a word jumped into her mind, and she wrote it down.

puddle

Which is what she felt like—a puddle of sweat. She wrote that whole phrase down.

a puddle of sweat

It was five syllables, the first line of a haiku . . . or the last line.

She kept writing, sort of free-associating, using the fingers of her left hand to tick off the syllables.

my mind is melting
my mind has melted
I am melted cheese
the school dissolves around me
the salty world dissolving
dissolving in salty drops
dissolving in saltiness-
I am dissolving
Heat melts my slow brain
Hot day melts my empty mind

> This day melting empty mind
> I am dissolving
> dissolves and slips down
> dissolves in slow drips

She started assembling different pieces, changing word forms to get the exact syllable count, trying to make seventeen syllables that felt right.

> A sweaty puddle,
> the heat melts the tired mind.
> I am dissolving.

She liked that last line—and noticed she'd written it several times. But the other stuff felt wrong. And she was liking the words "sweat" and "puddle" less and less. What would work?

Then she saw it and heard it and felt it all at the same moment, and she scribbled the words down just as Mr. Sanderling called time. The ten minutes had flown by.

"Okay," he said. "Copy one haiku onto your index card."

Jordan counted as he walked around and collected them. Only fourteen of the twenty-four kids in the class turned in a card.

Striding quickly to his desk, Mr. Sanderling pulled out his chair and stepped up onto the seat.

"And now," he announced with a booming voice, "let the great haiku competition begin!"

Even the snoozers sat up and listened as Mr. S. began. He was great at reading out loud.

Jordan thought several of the early contenders didn't even sound like poems—more like dull little newspaper reports.

> *Hot and humid air*
> *makes it harder to breathe right.*
> *Hot days are the worst.*

As Mr. S. kept going, Jordan was glad she had dropped the word "sweat." It appeared in five or six of the haiku, including the one that got the biggest laugh:

> *Heat has got me beat.*
> *My underwear is clammy.*
> *Sweat is not my friend.*

When hers was read aloud, Jordan really enjoyed the way it sounded. And she didn't care if anyone else liked it or not.

Drip by drop by droop,
steam heat melts my empty mind.
I am dissolving.

It turned out the other kids did like it. When the points were tallied, Reed Addison's clammy underwear haiku won first place, and Jordan's poem came in third, only a few points behind a really sweet one, the haiku she had liked best of all:

No war, no famine,
just a bit too warm today.
This isn't so bad.

Some of the kids clapped as Mr. Sanderling tapped out a fake drum roll on his desk, and she and Reed and Lindley Byrnes pulled their seats up to within a few feet of the fan. Jordan was impressed that Lindley had written such a thoughtful poem.

The cooler air felt great, but the respectful nod she got from Lindley was even better. She only wished Marlea had been there to see all this. And Kylie too. Of course, they'd hear about it at the next gathering of the Cuteness Club. . . .

Do I care if they hear about this? Or if anyone hears?

Jordan knew she *did* care.

Yes, it was just a little haiku, chosen from a tiny group of others that had all been slapped together in ten minutes.

Still, *she* was one of the winners. And she couldn't wait to tell Nikki.

CHAPTER FIFTEEN

IN THEIR BONES

The WCZF studios were located on County Road Seven, about three miles west of the Salton town center. The building was small, a thirty-foot square built of concrete blocks with a flat tar roof. The crisscrossed steel antenna tower rose up a hundred and ten feet into the air from its fenced area behind the parking lot. Six cables anchored it to the earth.

Inside there was a small reception area, a central workroom with four desks, and the two sound-proof broadcasting cubicles: one for country music programming and the other for the news, weather, and talk-radio programming.

Joe had spent most of the day studying the wide computer monitor on his desk in the workroom. On weekdays he spent two or three minutes on the air every half hour, from five a.m. to six thirty p.m.

This wasn't Joe's only job. He also taught an online meteorology course through the University of Illinois at Springfield, and he served every fourth weekend on a ground-support team with the 182nd Airlift Wing of the Illinois Air National Guard in Peoria.

But being the local weather guy in McLean County was the work he loved. He didn't tell the station manager, but he'd have done the job for free. It was endlessly interesting to him.

Some days it was also frustrating. Like today.

Warren hadn't called him back yet from the National Weather Service office. He really wanted some confirmation about the changes he was tracking in the local conditions. Or maybe he wanted an argument—or at least a discussion.

It was one thirty-four, so he had plenty of time before his next on-air report. Joe grabbed his water bottle and headed for the door. As he always told his students, a real meteorologist needs to get outside at least once every twelve hours. You had to walk around in the air mass and look up at the sky.

Passing through the double doors, he stepped onto the asphalt parking lot. It had been sixty-eight degrees inside, and out here it was up near ninety-five. By the time he had crossed the lot and walked fifty yards into the field behind the antenna, his shirt was wet. He felt like he was trying to breathe underwater.

Standing in the low grass, Joe turned a slow circle. The land here had been scraped flat by advancing and receding glaciers. The most recent ones had helped form a thick layer of some of the richest soil on the planet—soil soaked by recent rains. And today the Illinois prairie was exhaling. Water vapor caused a blurry haze that reached up ten degrees above the horizon in every direction. There was almost no breeze, but the dense air felt unsettled.

Or is that just my own mind, laying its views onto the conditions?

Weather forecasting was a tricky business.

But he *knew* weather like this. Growing up on his dad's farm, he had lived and worked through hundreds of days just like this one. And when the air was this warm and this saturated, and the sun was this bright, and the clouds were blooming, it was hard to miss the message. There was more to it than a bunch of numbers and some images on a computer screen.

Joe made a decision. It didn't matter if Warren

called him back or not. When he went on the air at 2:03 p.m., he was going to tell his local listeners to keep a real sharp eye on the sky.

But heck, they already knew that. Anybody working the land today could tell there was trouble coming. And they didn't need some supercomputer to figure it out.

They could feel it in their bones, same as he did.

CHAPTER SIXTEEN

ON THE BRAIN

Mrs. Lermon was glad to see that whatever had gotten Jordan so upset during homeroom this morning, it wasn't an issue anymore. She was practically glowing now—and not from the heat. The girl seemed happy.

Such a dear child!

It was good that Mrs. Lermon couldn't read minds, or she might have changed that opinion. One reason Jordan looked so happy? She'd just figured out that after today, there would be only two more science classes this year. Tuesday's all-school assembly would kill one, Field Day would kill another, and the last day of school was morning only.

Science makes me nuts. . . .

Jordan thought a second, tapping her fingers on the table. . . . Yup, five syllables.

Thanks to Mr. Sanderling, she now had a bad case of haiku–itis.

Also called haiku fever . . . which was seven syllables.

She enjoyed knowing some of the stuff they studied in science, especially the earth sciences and outer space stuff. But all the lab work? It reminded her of chess—lots of rules, tons of little steps, and everything had to be planned out in advance.

My brain is rotting away. . . .

Seven syllables . . . *aargh!*

But Nikki loved science, every bit of it. And if Nikki hadn't been her lab partner, Jordan knew she would have probably gotten Ds all year instead of Cs.

Of course, she'd have to deal with science again and again, all during junior high and high school. . . . Maybe it would seem easier later on. Jordan frowned.

That seems unlikely. . . .

Which was five syllables.

Anyway, two more classes, and science would vanish for three months.

Mrs. Lermon stepped to the chalkboard and wrote four words:

barometer
hygrometer
thermometer
anemometer

"Eyes front, everyone . . . thank you. Today we're reviewing a unit we studied back in February. What earth science do these four words relate to? Show of hands . . ."

Seven or eight hands went up, and Mrs. Lermon called on Leonard Sasken.

"Weather."

Mrs. Lermon nodded. "And the science of weather is called . . ."

"Meteorology."

"Good. Now," she went on, "each of these words ends with a two-syllable suffix that means what?"

She scanned the hands and pointed. "Annie?"

"To measure."

"Right. Think of a meter stick. And who can recall which weather elements these different devices measure?"

Jordan lost interest. She knew the answers: barometric pressure, humidity, temperature, and wind speed. She'd done okay on that unit. Her garden wasn't huge, but she cared about it, so she paid attention to the weather. She had to.

When spring rains come down,
The soil whispers, Thank you . . .

Did "soil" count as one syllable or two?

Soil . . . soil . . .

Two springs ago, her mom had helped her build a small display stand next to the end of their driveway. It was just some white-painted boards laid across two sawhorses, shaded by a large blue-and-orange U of I umbrella. She had painted two sandwich-board signs that stood out beside the road from April to November—HOMEGROWN FOODS. She grew and sold everything from asparagus to zucchini, and fresh flowers, too—not large quantities, but high quality. Between fifty and seventy-five cars and trucks drove past their house each afternoon on County Road Twelve, and loyal customers stopped several times a week. So far she had put more than six hundred dollars in the bank.

She was thinking of buying a small power tiller and using it to expand her pumpkin patch. Pumpkins brought in good money, and the deer and raccoons left them alone—as long as there were plenty of other munchies around . . . but Shep, their border collie, kept most of the critters away.

Of course, Shep had been known to chew on the veggies too. . . .

The deer and raccoons
Will share my garden with Shep.
Nature is messy.

"And this digital hygrometer? The measurement is expressed as a percentage. Who can tell me why? No one? Well, it's because air that is totally saturated with as much water vapor as it can hold without precipitation is represented by . . ."

Jordan kept her eyes forward, but tuned out again. Mrs. Lermon had this way of asking question after question, and she answered half of them herself. Her little lectures could fill a whole class period. Which seemed to be what was happening. Plus, it was like the teachers had gotten together and said, "In every class today, how about we all do things related to this weather, so no one has any chance of forgetting how hot and muggy it is. Hey, sounds like fun!"

It wasn't. What she *didn't* need right now was a detailed explanation of the respiratory and integumentary discomfort caused by dew points above sixty-eight degrees Fahrenheit.

Jordan glanced over at Nikki. She was taking notes like crazy, acting like every word Mrs. Lermon said was a gift of brilliance.

Maybe Mr. Graisha would cancel the after-school orchestra practice. . . .

No, no way. He was going to drill them on that thumping graduation music over and over and over. The man was sort of insane.

The man was insane. . . .

Five syllables.

She thought Nikki would have been more excited when she'd told her about being one of the haiku winners. Nikki had smiled and said, "Really? That's great!" But that was it. It had sort of slapped her back to reality.

After all, Nikki had actually *done* most of what she had only wished about doing this year. Nikki had had a speaking role in the school play, she'd been a wingback on the soccer team and a guard on the basketball team, she played first chair viola in the orchestra, and she had performed her own modern dance routine in the April Fool's Day talent show.

And with all the different ways there were to stand out, to be special, to make something of herself, what had *Jordan* done this year? She'd won twelve minutes of sitting in front of a clicking fan that smelled like burning plastic.

And now she had haiku on the brain.

I have haiku on the brain. . . .

Seven syllables.

So what could she do? Not much.

Set simple goals.

One: live through the rest of this class.

Two: live through the orchestra practice—and try to avoid Marlea.

Three: go home and water her tomato plants and sweet corn.

And maybe take Cinders out for a slow ride through the woods . . . and stop and go wading in the stream.

She sighed. The next-to-next-to-last science class . . .

Next-to-next-to-last . . .

Five syllables.

CHAPTER SEVENTEEN

VELVET AND STEEL

The orchestra was twenty minutes into the practice, and Jordan thought it was going pretty well. Mr. Graisha had broken up the piece into sections, and they were playing each section three times before adding the next one.

Also, instead of waving his little white baton around, he was clapping his hands to mark the rhythm and at the same time singing out the melody of *Pomp and Circumstance* at the top of his lungs.

"Daa, da da da daa daa, daa, da da da daaaa!"

The man looked totally insane, but it was working.

It was just as hot and humid in the auditorium building as it had been over in the main school all day. Mr. Graisha's face was bright red, and he was sweating buckets, but he hardly seemed to notice.

"All right," he shouted, "this time I want to hear the first twenty measures, the whole theme, right up to the first big crescendo—and play it *loud*, okay? Fill up the whole auditorium, blow the roof off the joint!"

He began clapping. "Okay, here we go! And one, and two, and, Daaa, da da da daaa daaa, daaa da da da . . ."

He stopped singing and waved his hands over his head.

"Hold it!" he shouted. "Hold it—someone's really out of tune—*stop playing!* Stop! Everyone!"

The orchestra stumbled to a halt, but the harsh tone that had thrown him off kept droning on. It was from outside.

Mr. Graisha hurried over to the wide double doors facing the playground and pushed the right one open. A burst of wind slammed the door right back, and it hit him hard. He staggered backward, then dropped to his knees, stunned. Then he slowly toppled to his side and lay still, one foot still holding the door ajar. Another burst of wind ripped the door open and knocked it back against the outside of the building—WHAM, WHAM, WHAM! A playground trash barrel sailed in through the open door, two feet above

Mr. Graisha. It tumbled once and clattered onto the hardwood floor of the stage, spilling paper and empty plastic bottles everywhere.

Above the sound of the wind and the whamming door, the original noise kept going. It was the town emergency siren.

Only a few seconds had passed, and the kids still sat glued to their chairs, instruments in their hands. Then, as if they were puppets all connected by the same string, everyone jumped up. Kids began yelling, and some were screaming. "What do we do? What do we do? We've got to get to the school!"

Somebody's cello hit the floor. Its neck broke, and the strings made a sickly twang.

Jordan knew in a flash. This was a thunderstorm. Or even a tornado. Her breaths turned to short gasps. She felt fear clutching at her throat, making her want to scream.

NO!

She tried to think.

WhatdoIdo, whatdoIdo, whatdoIdo, whatdoIdo?

A shiny set of words jumped into her mind, words she'd said to herself just minutes ago, at the end of science class.

Set simple goals, right?

First, Mr. Graisha.

She could see a huge bump on his forehead. And blood. But she also saw he was breathing.

We have to get him away from there.

Sudden pain shot through her hands—her violin and bow, gripped tightly, all her knuckles white. On pure instinct, she bent down and put the instrument in the case, clicking all three clasps.

Her head jerked up as both doors on the west side of the stage slammed open, pushed outward by the wind from the playground side. Leaves, grass, paper, sticks, part of a wooden fence—it was like the whole outside world was trying to rush into the building. Raw, angry noise filled every bit of space, howling and whistling and growling, and it kept getting louder.

A four-foot strip of blue-and-yellow plastic clattered in through the playground door, whacked against Mr. Graisha's foot, and tumbled all the way across the stage. Part of Jordan's mind realized it was a piece of the spiral sliding board.

The kids were huddled in little groups now, some with tears streaming down their faces—especially the younger ones. Jordan felt like she was trapped in a dream and couldn't wake up.

She jumped as someone grabbed her elbow.

Nikki put her mouth next to Jordan's ear and yelled, "We need help!"

Jordan had never seen Nikki scared of anything, not in all the time they'd known each other. Right now her eyes were open so wide, she looked like an anime character. She was beyond scared.

Jordan was scared too, but she fought the fear. It tried to paralyze her, tried to make her dizzy and weak. It felt exactly like a bad dream, so she forced herself to wake up, forced herself to think. The fear didn't go away, but the whole scene snapped into focus, more vivid than a 3-D movie. And she saw what had to happen.

She took Nikki's hand and yelled, "Stay close!"

Jordan pulled Nikki and ran over to the grand piano. She grabbed her book bag, reached into the small pocket, and a second later, she sucked in a huge breath and blew three sharp whistle blasts. *Breet! Breet! Breet!*

The sound of that Acme Thunderer cut through the noise of the wind, the screams and whimpers of the kids, and the wailing siren.

Every kid on the stage turned to look at Jordan.

She blasted her whistle again and motioned for everyone to come close. In three seconds, twenty-two kids were gathered around her in a tight semicircle.

She yelled as loud as she could. "We have to hurry!" She pointed at Jonathan. "You and Rick and Susan and Ellie, get Mr. Graisha on that chair cart and roll him over here! Everyone else, grab the music stands and bring them next to the piano. And then the folding chairs! Hurry!"

No one moved. Nikki was still holding on to Jordan's arm.

Jordan put the whistle between her lips and blew it again. Nothing.

She stamped her feet. "Move!" The kids huddled closer.

She shouted again. *"HURRY, PLEASE!"*

Lindley moved first. She dashed to the center of the stage, grabbed two of the black music stands, and rushed back.

That broke the spell. Everyone jumped into action. In less than a minute, all twenty-three music stands were clustered around the big piano, and Jonathan and his team had wheeled Mr. Graisha over. Nikki came back to life, and she and Kylie and Marlea led a brigade that gathered all the folding chairs.

Jordan motioned that Mr. Graisha's rolling cart had to be tight against the long, straight side of the piano. Then she took hold of one of the music stands and tilted the top part flat, like the top of a *T*. She motioned and yelled, "All of them, like this! Hurry, *please*!"

As eight or ten kids began that job, she grabbed Jonathan's arm and shouted into his ear. "Get a bunch of kids!" She motioned for him to follow.

She ran to where half the curtain hung folded along the wall of the stage. Reaching above her head, she grabbed the edge of the thick fabric.

The noise outside now sounded like giant jet engines, whistling and whining. In the auditorium, the high windows on the west wall began bursting inward, and glass shattered onto the seats.

Jordan screamed, *"Everybody grab hold! One, two, three, PULL!"*

Seven kids yanked hard and then hung on the edge of the curtain.

For a second nothing happened, then far above, the cloth gave way, and a massive wave of red velvet cascaded to the floor. A dust cloud vanished in the swirling air.

Jordan seized the corner of the fabric closest to the wall and pantomimed how the others needed to grab it along the front edge and stretch it wide. Then she led the charge, pointing to show them what to do.

They pulled the wide billow of velvet like a rain tarp across a baseball field, and in one smooth flow, the seven kids hauled it up and over the tops of the music stands and the folding chairs and the rolling chair cart and the grand piano.

And that was it.

Jordan blew the whistle and motioned with her arms.

Instantly, everyone understood what to do. Jordan ran out to the center of the stage, grabbed her violin case, then dropped to her knees and followed the last two kids under the curtain.

The wind noise rose again to a higher pitch, and one of the stage doors facing the playground banged twice, then ripped off its hinges and sailed sixty feet straight across the back of the stage like a giant rectangular Frisbee. It slammed against the far doors and knocked the whole metal frame out onto the concrete steps.

Jordan heard the sounds and felt the sudden change in air pressure as all that happened, but she didn't see any of it. By then she was with Mr. Graisha and the rest of the orchestra, hidden inside their steel and velvet fort.

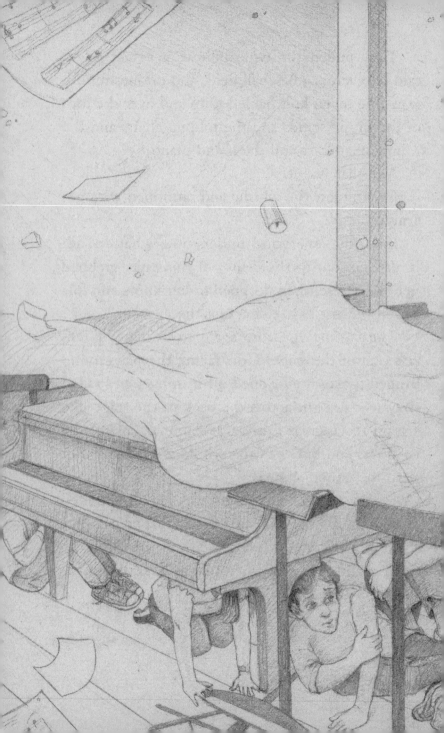

CHAPTER EIGHTEEN

SOS

J oe Streeter was one of the first people at the scene, arriving shortly after the fire trucks and police cars. He'd never seen a tornado this powerful whip up so fast—an F2 or even an F3, by the look of things. A sudden clash of forces and temperature gradients, then a deep wind shear and a massive rotation—six minutes from start to finish.

The path of the twister made no sense at all, not that any of them ever did. Early eyewitnesses said it had snaked across some fields west of town, lifted clean over the downtown, touched down and destroyed two homes a block apart in the Jerome Gardens subdivision, and then hopped six blocks and landed right on the playground at Baird Elementary.

The main building only had some minor glass

damage, plus the boiler chimney on the east wall had toppled into the bus turnaround. The school had been nearly empty—only nine students and fourteen staff and faculty members. There wasn't a storm cellar, but everyone had gotten to the designated inner hallway space in time. There hadn't been a single injury, and all were accounted for.

But Joe stood with Carl Tretorn, the fire chief, staring at the auditorium building. A large brick structure, it had stood just forty feet away from the main building. The connecting walkway was perfectly intact, its roof and columns untouched, while the auditorium itself was nearly flattened. All that remained standing were a few steel girders that had supported the frame of the stage.

"I tell you what," Carl said, nodding toward the rubble. "We lucked out on this one, big-time. The boiler's over in the other building, so there were no broken gas lines, and there was nothing scheduled for after school. Flipped one big breaker and cut all the electricity. Every once in a while you catch a break."

He eyed Joe. "So, was it you who triggered the sirens?"

Joe nodded. "Been watching all day. But you never think anything like this'll actually happen."

Carl spat onto the ground. "Well, a short warning's better than none, that's for darn sure. Nice work."

Joe nodded off to Carl's right. "Here comes Jim Regan. Is he still the principal here?"

Jim arrived at a run, his face the color of oatmeal. "The secretary," he said, panting, "she had a note on her blotter. There was a special orchestra practice in there. On the stage."

"Holy moly!" Carl turned and yelled to the men on the nearest trucks. "Survivors—north wall!"

The scene instantly transformed into a search-and-rescue operation. Picks and shovels appeared, and the chief got on the radio and ordered heavy equipment.

The first firefighter who trotted over and began tossing rubble aside suddenly stopped and held up one arm.

"*Quiet*—shut off those diesels!"

Joe pulled on a pair of borrowed gloves and stood still with the others. As a hush settled, he heard something too.

At first it sounded like a referee on a far-off basketball court, whistling a foul. Then he caught the pattern: three short blasts, three long, three short—*SOS*.

CHAPTER NINETEEN

APPLAUSE

A few things were unusual at the sixth-grade graduation the next Friday evening.

First, it was taking place in the auditorium at the new high school.

Second, the turnout was huge. Practically the whole town had showed up. Folks who couldn't fit into the hall were watching the live broadcast on the local cable channel.

And third, as the elementary school orchestra began playing *Pomp and Circumstance*, it was hard not to notice that the conductor was wearing something that looked like a white headband. It was a bandage.

As Jordan had predicted, the superintendent's speech included these words: "After all, this certainly isn't an ending. It is more like a great beginning."

But no one could have predicted what happened after Caroline Jenkins received her certificate of completion and sat back down.

Because when Jordan Johnston's name was called, and she rose and walked across the stage, every single person in the large hall stood up and began to applaud. Mr. Regan had her certificate, but he didn't hand it to her. He was clapping too, and he smiled and motioned for her to turn and face the audience.

Jordan looked out and saw so many faces she knew. Her mom and dad were there in the front row, and her sister, Allie, was holding up her little brother, Tim, so he could see. She saw the Carvers and three or four other families and lots of kids who knew her as their babysitter. She saw people who had stopped and bought sunflowers and carrots and green beans at her roadside stand. She saw all her teachers, waving and smiling at her.

And from the corner of her eye, she saw her classmates clapping and cheering like crazy—including Marlea Harkins.

Jordan smiled back at everyone and then stepped forward to the front edge of the stage and took a deep, graceful bow.

Mr. Regan walked to her side and held up a

hand until the hall went quiet. Everyone remained standing.

The principal turned to Jordan. "In addition to your certificate of completion, the school board wants to present you with a special commendation, and I shall now read it."

He perched his glasses on the tip of his nose and began:

"The duly elected school board of Salton, Illinois, does hereby commend Jordan Eloise Johnston for her outstanding bravery, her clear thinking, and her decisive actions during a devastating tornado that struck the Baird Elementary School on June 14. In only four minutes, Jordan implemented a safety plan and devised a hiding place that protected her own life, the lives of twenty-two other children, and the life of her orchestra conductor, who had been knocked unconscious. What almost certainly would have been a great and scarring tragedy has instead become this wonderful occasion to offer Jordan the heartfelt thanks of a grateful community. We remain forever in her debt."

This time the applause went on and on, continuing even after Jordan had gone back to her seat.

No one rushed to the stage to push two dozen

yellow roses into her arms, there were no auto-graph seekers and no paparazzi.

But none of that mattered.

Jordan, Plain and Average, was completely happy about everything, including herself.

Acknowledgments

I want to thank the people at the National Weather Service for the wealth of meteorological information they make available online. I also need to make it clear that the events imagined in this fictional story are in no way meant to reflect poorly upon the remarkable job the National Weather Service does every day to provide warning to the public about approaching dangers.

I also wish to thank my editor, Caitlyn Dlouhy, and all the other fine professionals at Atheneum Books for Young Readers for helping me to seem smarter, more grammatical, more logical, and more consistent than I actually am. (And yes, I'm sure they've even checked over these brief acknowledgments with great care!)

I want to offer particular thanks to Amy Berkower at Writers House for her wise counsel and support.

—A. C.

A Reading Group Guide for

ABOUT AVERAGE

by Andrew Clements

ABOUT THE BOOK

Jordan Johnston wishes she were extraordinarily popular, pretty, athletic, musical, intelligent . . . something! She dreams about escaping her average existence, but what she can't figure out is exactly how. Then nature intervenes, and Jordan discovers something way above average about herself that may have been there all along.

DISCUSSION TOPICS

1. From the start of the novel, it is clear that Jordan is frustrated by her lack of special talents. Reread the first ten pages of the novel and then list at least four things at which Jordan appears to have skill. Can you think of a word or phrase to describe the types of aptitudes Jordan possesses? What kind of "above average" abilities does she want?

2. What does Marlea Harkins do that upsets Jordan? What options does Jordan consider to retaliate

against Marlea? Do you agree with her thought process? What advice would you give to Jordan at the end of Chapter Four?

3. At the end of Chapter Six, Jordan observes that: "Numbers were so clean and simple. No words, no feelings, no mind tricks. Numbers were like a hiding place, a quiet corner out of the wind." Do you feel this way about numbers, or can you understand what Jordan means? Is there another school subject or activity that brings you comfort? Explain your answer.

4. Who is "Joe the Weather Guy"? What gives Joe a bit of extra insight into the weather in central Illinois?

5. How does Jordan feel when she overhears her parents discussing her abilities? Have you ever had the experience of hearing adults discuss your academic, athletic, or artistic skills, or your future? How did you react to this experience?

6. Who are Jordan's good friends? How does she relate to these friends? Who are the members of the Cuteness Club, why are they called that, and how do they intersect with Jordan's group of friends? Do you think Jordan should have discussed the Marlea situation with one of her friends? Why or why not?

7. What ingenious idea does Jordan finally have for dealing with Marlea? What is your opinion of this idea? Do you think you could pull it off? What possible reactions could you envision for treating difficult people in your school or community with "extra niceness"?

8. What is Jordan's genius babysitting trick? How does this trick show Jordan's insights into kids and people in general? How does it foreshadow her actions later in the story?

9. What contest does Jordan win in Mr. Sanderling's class? How does Jordan feel about the win? Is it enough to satisfy her need to be "not average"?

10. What does Joe feel in his bones in Chapter Fifteen? Can you find evidence in the chapter that others also have a sense of foreboding about the weather? What decision does Joe make?

11. Why is Mr. Graisha's decision to hold the after-school rehearsal in the auditorium building a bad one? What happens shortly after the rehearsal begins? What happens to the teacher? How do the other kids react?

12. How does Jordan's earlier decision to set simple goals affect her own reaction to the weather situation? What does she do?

13. Does Jordan's dream of being applauded by her community come true in the way she imagined? What happens at sixth-grade graduation?
14. Is Jordan really average at all? Is anyone?

ACTIVITIES AND RESEARCH

1. Use an online dictionary to find the multipart definition of the word "average." Write at least six sentences using the term in different ways and/or different parts of speech. Write a paragraph describing a fictional average student, athlete, singer, or other type of person.
2. Create an informative poster describing the study of meteorology, including how one becomes a meteorologist and a list of at least four jobs meteorologists can do other than being a television or radio weather person. With friends or classmates discuss whether you would consider a career in meteorology.
3. In the character of Marlea, write a journal entry from her point of view, describing what happened the morning she read Jordan's list in the bathroom. Or, with friends or classmates, role-play the bathroom scene with Jordan, Marlea, and the girls to whom she reads the list (improvising their reactions), and a scene in

which Marlea tells Kylie what she did and Kylie reacts (this scene is not in the actual novel).

4. Jordan feels that Marlea's actions toward her are bullying. Do you agree or disagree? Write a paragraph defining the term "bullying" and, if necessary, discussing how you might categorize other types of unacceptable school behavior.

5. Describe the plans in place to help kids handle bullying situations at Jordan's school. Does your school have an anti-bullying policy? If it does, compare your plan to that of Jordan's school. If not, brainstorm a plan to propose to your teacher and principal.

6. With friends or classmates, make a wall-sized poster or mural depicting things at which you excel, such as soccer, spelling, petsitting, etc. Write a few words describing each ability in colorful lettering and illustrate them with images of you and your friends in action.

7. Survey friends, family, or classmates about whether they use lists for decision making, to remember things, for shopping, for schoolwork, or for other reasons. Have they ever had difficulty with a list getting into the wrong hands? What is the most important list they have ever made? Create a graph or chart summarizing your survey results.

8. Jordan decides to deal with the Marlea situation using kindness. Spend a few hours or even an entire school day using only kind words in your interactions with friends, classmates, and teachers. Afterward, write a journal entry describing the experience, noting whether this behavior affected your mood, concentration, or schoolwork. If desired, share your observations with friends or classmates.

9. The weather plays a critical role in the novel. Write two to three paragraphs describing the climate of your hometown. Be sure to include some notes on the most dangerous types of weather you experience in your region. For one week, start each day by stepping outside your front door and then writing down your best guess at the kind of weather the day will bring. Then take note of the daily weather report given on your local television or radio station or online. At the end of each day, compare the professional forecast and your guess to the actual weather of the day.

10. Have you ever experienced a hurricane, tornado, blizzard, severe heat wave, or other dangerous weather situation? Write a short story describing this experience.

11. Find out whether your family, school, and community have plans to deal with dangerous weather situations. Visit the National Oceanic and Atmospheric Administration online at nws.noaa.gov/com/weatherreadynation to learn more about making a weather emergency plan for your area. Encourage friends and classmates to educate themselves about weather preparedness.

12. You are the person assigned to create Jordan's special commendation. Use a graphic design computer program and be sure to include the wording noted in the final chapter of the novel.

Guide written by Stasia Kehoe

This guide has been provided by Simon & Schuster for classroom, library, and reading group use. It may be reproduced in its entirety or excerpted for these purposes.

IN THE HILLS
ABOVE KABUL

Sadeed knew he wasn't supposed to be listening to the men talking in the next room. He also knew he wasn't supposed to be peeking through the crack near the bottom of the old wooden door. But they had to be talking about him in there—why else would his teacher have invited him to the home of the headman of the village?

His teacher, Mahmood Jafari, had not told him much. "Please come to Akbar Khan's house this afternoon at four. He and his councillors meet today, and I have to speak with them. And I may need you to be there."

Sadeed thought perhaps his teacher was going to recommend him for a special honor. That wasn't hard to imagine, not at all. Perhaps the village elders would award him a scholarship to one of the finest new schools in Kabul. He would wear blue trousers and a clean white shirt to classes every day, and he would have his own computer, and he would take his place as one of the future leaders of Afghanistan. His father and mother would be very proud of him. It would be a great opportunity. And Sadeed was certain he richly deserved it.

Through the crack in the door, Sadeed could see all seven men, sitting on cushions around a low table, sipping tea. An electric bulb hung overhead, and two wires ran across the ceiling to the gasoline generator outside. Mahmood was talking to Akbar Khan, but the teacher's back was toward the door, and Sadeed couldn't hear what he was saying.

When the teacher finished, someone Sadeed knew—Hassan Jaji—began to speak. Hassan stopped by his father's shop in the village bazaar at least once a week, and he sometimes stayed awhile, telling stories about his time as a freedom fighter during the war with the Soviet Union. One day he had shown Sadeed where a Russian grenade had blown two fingers off his right hand.

And as the man spoke now, that was the hand he used to stroke his chin.

"I am only a simple man," Hassan said, "and I would never try to stop progress. But our traditions protect us. And they protect our children. And I believe that the schoolteacher has asked us to allow something that would not be proper."

The eyes of the men turned back to Mahmood. The teacher looked around the circle and cleared his throat, speaking more forcefully now so that Sadeed could hear every word he said. "What Hassan says about our traditions is certainly true."

He paused, and Sadeed saw him hold up a bright green envelope with three stamps on it, each one a small picture of an American flag. The front of the envelope was decorated with two pink butterfly stickers.

The teacher said, "But it is also a tradition that we are a courteous people. And therefore one student from our village school must answer this letter from the girl in America. And I believe it would be *most* courteous if our very best student writes back, the one student who is most skillful with the English language. And that one student is Sadeed Bayat."

A pang of disappointment cut through Sadeed.

His name had just been spoken in the ears of the most important men in this part of Panjshir Province, and why? To be recommended for a great honor? No. To write a letter. To a girl.

Hassan stroked his chin again. He shook his head. "That letter is from an American girl. And should a boy and a girl be sharing their thoughts this way? No. Let one of the girls write back. A girl would be more proper."

And outside the door, Sadeed nodded and whispered, "Exactly!"

The teacher spoke up again. "To be sure, what Hassan says would be best. But the letter that goes back to America will represent our village, even our nation. And should we accept less than the very best writing, the best spelling and grammar? I know Sadeed Bayat—you may know him too, the son of Zakir the wheat merchant. He is a good boy. And his excellent writing will represent us well. His words will speak well of all the children of Afghanistan. And I feel sure that no harm will come of this. I feel sure that—"

Akbar Khan held up a hand, and Mahmood went silent.

The headman said, "Have you told Sadeed about this letter yet?"

"No," said the teacher. "I came to ask for advice."

Akbar nodded. "You did well to wait." The headman looked around the circle. "I agree that the finest student from our village must reply. And I agree that it would be best if a girl from our school is the writer." Akbar turned to the teacher. "Sadeed has a sister, doesn't he?"

"Yes," Mahmood said. "Amira, about two years younger."

The headman smiled. "Just so. Amira will write back to the girl in America. And the finest student from our village will watch over her and help her, doing what is needed to be sure that the writing is excellent. But only the girl will sign the letter. And therefore, all will be proper. And, of course, our teacher promises that nothing shameful will come of this." Looking Mahmood full in the face, he said, "Do you promise this?"

Mahmood nodded. "I do."

"Then it is decided," said Akbar Khan. "And now we will have more tea."

Fifteen minutes later, when his teacher came out into the entry hall, Sadeed was sitting on the long wooden bench with two men who had arrived to speak before the village elders. He stood up and followed his teacher down the hallway, out the door, across the walled courtyard, and then through the iron gate that opened onto the main road.

As they stood beside the road, Mahmood smiled and said, "Thank you for coming, Sadeed. It turns out that I needn't have bothered you. I know you need to hurry to your job now, but I must speak with you before school tomorrow morning. I need your help with an important job."

Sadeed nodded, taking care to put a puzzled look on his face.

"So," Mahmood said. "Good evening."

And with a small, formal bow, the teacher turned right and walked toward the school, headed home. Not only did he work at the school, but he lived in a room built against the rear wall of the building.

Sadeed turned in the other direction, headed back toward the bazaar. He worked for his father every day after school, and the shop would be open for at least another hour.

As he walked along the road, following a large man riding on a small donkey, he thought about all he had heard. No great honors were heading his way. However, Akbar Khan himself had called him "the finest student from our village." So that was good.

And Sadeed also thought about tomorrow, about how he would have to pretend to be surprised when his teacher told him he must help Amira—just like he had pretended to be puzzled a few moments ago.

But the only thing that actually puzzled Sadeed was how his teacher could call writing a letter to a girl in America "an important job."

Because *that* made no sense at all.